VALENTINE

JADE EBY

KENYA WRIGHT

VALENTINE

JADE EBY

KENYA WRIGHT

To all the underrated heroes who need just as much love as the rest of us.

PROLOGUE

CUPID

When the full moon hovered over Asher's home, no glow rained down.

Just shadows and fake light.

Darkness on clouds.

The property dimmed. Crickets made no sound. Owls did not hoot. The wind ran cold. Tree branches scraped against the top windows of the mansion, sounding like the cries of heartbroken women.

And in the air, the fragrance of death lingered.

Far off in the distance, police combed Ovid Island for a serial killer, some dark man that had just killed his fifth millionaire, carved a name into the latest victim's chest, and left a bloody message for Diana Carson.

Sirens blared.

Throughout the night, helicopters rose from the island and sped off with fearful and wicked rich men that were smart enough to know they might be next and should escape while they can.

Within the shadows of his mansion, Asher sat in his private office and drowned in glasses of Brandy aged for years in oak and providing his taste buds with a rich caramel flavor. The bottle ran him thousands of dollars. He had planned to open it on a special day.

Instead, that night, Asher took the bottle out to drown in misery, while he thought of all the things that had gone wrong.

"Right now, you are my lover, and friend," he'd just said to Diana hours earlier. *"But if you try to escape, if you point me out to the police as Cupid, I will no longer be your friend."*

Diana glared back in defiance. "I don't believe you."

"That's not a risk you want to take with me. My hand is skilled, when I hold my bow. It does not shake. My arrow hits the target. It will not waver."

He'd gone too far. That was what the brandy whispered as he swam all through its rough waves. Insecurities popped into his head. Worries wrestled each other in his brain, and deep inside of him the hunger for blood rose.

Asher tried to drink it all away and think of better things.

She loves me. She loves me not.

His body descended into the pool of alcohol,

falling,

down,

down,

down to the bottom of each glass.

She loves me. She loves me not, and what would I do, if she doesn't love me?

Sighing, he swallowed more, dropping even further, maybe even beyond the hard glass and merging somewhere in between reality and a dream state. Or maybe it was more of a nightmare.

Even earlier that night, he'd pulled his cock out of Diana's lovely warmth and it dripped with her arousal. He couldn't help himself, turned her over, took her jaw in his hands, and brought her face close to him.

"I'm not like any man you've ever known," he'd said. "I'm your favorite nightmare and your worst dream all in one. I'm everything you shouldn't want. And you're everything I need. Everything I don't deserve."

His office door opened and he blinked to make sure he wasn't seeing things.

Asher's mother walked toward him, dripping in pearls and rubies, still wearing her fur coat. He'd forced her to go to Paris. He'd needed her out of the mansion, before Diana moved in. The whole living arrangement with Diana was supposed to be temporary, a few weeks of sex and mental games. He'd planned to move on to another kill, after his fun with her. By then, Diana would've been off his property and writing about something else besides Cupid, and his mother would return.

He blew out a long breath. "Why are you back so early?"

"You told her everything? This Diana Carson. That

reporter." His mother ruffled her blonde waves with jeweled fingers. "Why would you do that, Asher?"

"How do you know?"

She took off her coat, slung it against the couch near the door, and dropped her purse on the floor. "How do I always know? I'm your mother. Why? Why would you tell her everything?"

"She found out the truth on her own. I left her in my bedroom. She went into my closet and discovered the bow and arrow. She wanted something to wear because she was... naked... " He lifted the glass of brandy to his lips and finished it whole. "What else could I do?"

Diana's lush curves and smooth brown skin spun through his mind and knocked away all his insecurities and worries.

I'm doing the right thing. She's mine.

"Did you hear anything I said?" Asher's mother stomped over to his desk, the one she'd bought years ago on one of her many trips to Paris. She'd loved that city, the lush vibrancy of the streets and how the glow of culture and history swelled from its ancient bricks. Traveling was the only thing that kept her happy for a few days.

"Asher?!"

"What?"

"You're not listening to me."

He burped. "Go right ahead, Dear Mother."

"You've made a mess of everything." She raised her hands in the air. On her charm bracelet, diamond hearts clinked against each other and rung over and over. The noise flooded his head, almost blocking out some of the words that spilled out of her mouth. "You have me go on this trip to do what? Romance a reporter that is investigating your murders. And even worse, one of your victims was her husband—"

"She didn't love him anymore."

"How would you even know this?"

"It was obvious. Plus, we've made love."

His mother sucked her teeth. "This woman is in shock and mourning the death of her husband. It doesn't matter if she had sex with you. Widows have done worse things while dealing with tragic deaths. I was a widow several times. Widows don't think while they mourn. They just do."

"How would you know?" Asher picked up the crystal decanter next to him, took off the top, and poured more brandy into his glass. "You've never really been a mourning widow. A widow, sure, but not a sad one."

"I've read books on the mourning process. I learned the proper way to act, which was basically erratic and emotional." His mother placed her hands on her hips. "And there was never any need to mourn my ex-husbands, they were all bad men, and my son saved me from them."

Asher raised a blonde eyebrow. "Were my step-fathers really bad?"

"Not this again! I didn't lie all of those times. I've never lied. Those men really did do bad things to me." She touched her chest. "I am not a monster. What type of woman would make up horrible things so that her son would take her husbands' lives?"

"One that wanted to be a rich woman."

She shrugged and tousled her hair some more. "I've never needed to have money. I've just been lucky enough that the bad men I meet, well... they've been rich."

"Not my father."

She snapped her attention to him and glared. "Do. Not. Discuss. Him."

"Calm down." Sighing, he took a big gulp of brandy.

"Now you're going to have to kill her."

He almost spat out the liquor, but instead coughed several times to clear his airways.

"Just go up there right now. She's here, right? In this house, upstairs, in one of *our* rooms?" His mother frowned. "I can do it for you this time. What would make you feel better about this? Pills? Your bow and arrow? A knife? Knives are so messy, but you've always loved the sight of blood. I can't touch the stuff. It makes me want to vomit—"

"Shut up!" Asher slammed his closed fist onto the desk. "I'm not going to do anything to Diana."

"No?" His mother tossed him an evil grin.

"No."

"Don't kill her, then. That's a great idea." She clapped her hands and plastered on a fake smile. "Oh goodie. You and she will just go off in the sunset. I've always wanted a lovely daughter-in-law, and maybe we can plan a summer wedding. How glorious!" His mother mocked and did a dramatic twirl. "Asher and his scared bride walking down the aisle. Will you have blood on your hands during the ceremony? Make sure you wash them first. You'll probably kill someone right before the ceremony. You can't deny your hunger. Wash those hands. You don't want to get all of that red on her lovely white gown. You don't want to terrify her even more—"

"She's not afraid of me."

His mother pierced him with a deadly gaze. "She will be. I was afraid of you."

"You made me what I am."

"That didn't stop me from being terrified."

Although he should've ignored his mother, the statement broke his heart, twisted the beating muscle into a knotted mess. "You should've been scared. You had me kill your husbands over your stupid lies. Dirty things that you knew would get me angry enough to kill them. If I'm a monster, you made me that way, through your lies to a loyal son. You. Made. Me. This. Way."

"No." She pointed her finger at me. "I *helped* you. You loved it. Every damn minute. Don't forget. You told me that you hungered for the sight of blood. You dreamt about it. My lies to a loyal son? No, my sick son, one who can never walk hand-in-hand into the sunset with any woman because he just might kill her—"

"Shut up!" His vision blurred a little. His mother's image rippled and then returned to a clear view. Perhaps, it was the liquor. He'd been on his fifth glass when his mother waltzed into his office.

"Wake up!" She clapped. "Wake up, son, and smell the roses."

In that moment, Diana's rosy scent swarmed all around him. He'd even sniffed between those thighs, dipping the point of his nose into her warm pussy and breathed in that lovely flower.

"Maybe smelling the roses is my problem," he muttered.

"You're going to have to kill Diana Carson."

"No."

"That wasn't a question, my dear. It's the reality of the situation."

"No."

"Gut that reporter bitch! I want her blood all over this carpet. Fuck her while you do it, if you want to. I don't care. Just do it." His mother smoothed a wrinkle on her silk shirt. "Have you ever done that? Fucked while you killed? I bet it's quite the erotic experience."

Asher slumped in his chair. The room twisted into a sort of slow motion as if he sat in the center of a merry-go-round. His hand shook, as he brought the brandy to his mouth. And the whole time his mother talked, his cock got hard, thinking of Diana's opened legs and the scent of blood.

His mother clapped again. "You, my son, were born a monster."

"You made me this way."

"If you are right, then you have to admit that something inside of you is wrong."

"No, Mother. I know something is wrong with me. We just disagree on the origin." He poured another glass and got ready to swallow that one whole.

"How long have you been drinking?" She snatched the glass from his hands.

Asher blinked with confusion. The glass still sat in his fingers, yet, in front of him his mother stood, nagging and holding the very same glass in her hand.

Two glasses, when there had only been one.

How drunk am I? What's going on? Were there two glasses? Didn't she take mine? It's in her hand right now. But it's also in mine.

He blinked again.

"Stop drinking and deal with this problem." His mother slung the glass behind her. It hit the floor and shattered into tiny pieces.

But, when Asher turned to his hand, that same glass remained in his grip. He let out a long breath and returned to his mother's rippling image. "This isn't real."

The shattered glass appeared right back in her hands as if she'd never slung it. Laughter fled her lips. She hurled it at him. He ducked. The glass propelled into the air. Yet, once he blinked, nothing happened.

It all disappeared.

His mother's image faded in and out. "Our conversations are never real, darling."

"Oh yes. I forgot. I killed you. Didn't I?"

"Yes." His mother nodded.

"Because in the end, I found out the kind of woman you really are. A lying, selfish bitch. Those husbands of yours were innocent, and I wouldn't let you force me to take anymore people's lives that didn't deserve it."

"Oh bravo." She gave him a standing ovation. "Let's be real. You killed me because you couldn't stand that mommy dearest knew you better than you knew yourself. You killed me and yet, you can't live without me, can you, Asher?"

"Stop it!" He yelled at the fading image of his mother.

Why am I arguing with a hallucination?

Because you're insane.

"This is not about me." She sashayed over to the couch. "This is about my lovely daughter-in-law sleeping upstairs."

"Go away, Mother."

"Fine, Asher." Her image blurred out a little, but her voice remained. "But we both know, that you'll kill Diana. There's no other way this can possibly work, and I'll be waiting to say, I told you so. And when you kill her, she'll haunt you as I do."

CHAPTER ONE

DIANA

Diana trembled.

Cupid.

Asher-Cupid.

A sick, gut-twisting curiosity stung at her heart. When Diana had found her babysitter in the backyard, that same feeling had consumed her.

She'd just been a young girl, hunting out clues. Instead of hidden treasure, Diana found death that day—cracked pink nails, a young face smashed on one side, twisted limbs, and burn marks where soft flesh should've been.

She didn't grab her parents for a reason. She wanted to show them how smart she'd become. If they saw how amazing she was, maybe they would stop all of the arguing about Dad losing his job. Maybe, they'd return back to normal—laughter and presents, giggling behind their closed bedroom door and movie nights where they all cuddled on the couch and wrapped each other in their love.

But nothing happened like her young mind had dreamed.

The police arrived, lifted the mutilated body from the ground, and arrested her father, the poor black man that owned the property.

Case closed.

Her dad spent the night in jail, and someone killed him for the crime. No one ever discovered his murderer. But then again, no one had bothered to try. He was merely a casualty in the prison war games.

A week later, the police discovered Gabby's actual killer, some dirty old man a few blocks away.

That event taught Diana two things: sometimes she could dig too much, and never ever trust the police to hand out true justice.

He's Cupid. So, what do I do now? I can't trust the police.

Once they returned home from his latest crime scene—the one where Asher had carved a message into a dead man—she took the sleeping pills from him like they were candy. Maybe she should have been more scared. Cautious to take anything from a man like him. But she swallowed the little white pills and the world spun around and swallowed her whole.

Barefoot and hungry, Diana stepped into a dream world that only Salvador Dali could've painted.

Desolate land stretched out for miles, a sea of hot, tan sand that continued as far as her eyes could see. It never ended, and no one appeared to be near her. An odd sky sat above with no sun or moon, just scattered light. Formless clouds faded into a distant darkness up ahead, where a full rainbow arched and seemed more trapped into the black.

She wore rusted armor over her chest. Underneath, a huge black gown fell to her feet and swished with the cruel wind. She also carried a wooden sword. It weighed heavy in her scarred hands.

"He's a murderer," she said to no one.

Something pushed Diana to move toward the rainbow, and she whispered again, "No. He's a vigilante. Dammit. I don't know what he is, but I want to."

Someone pulled up to her side.

Diana stopped and stared up at the most horrifying thing she'd seen in years. A skeleton sat on a horse with no skin or hair, just bones, teeth, and muscle.

"What is he to you?" the skeleton knight asked.

She drew her sword and pointed it at him. "Who are you talking about?"

"Cupid. Who is Cupid to you?"

The wooden sword trembled in her hands. "I'm not a cop, yet I've hunted down the vilest murderers and watched their lives leave their bodies on their days of executions."

The horse snorted and stomped its fleshy hooves.

The skeleton knight laughed. "So is he a killer?"

"I don't know."

"Come." The knight extended his bony hand.

She caught it and he lifted her in the air, the cold of him running straight through to her blood. She gritted her teeth, hopped on, and tried not to scream as she held onto his ribs. "Where are we going?"

"What is your name?"

"Don Quixote," she whispered.

"That is a beautiful name for a woman."

"Thank you."

They trotted off. Sand kicked up behind them. The world zipped by fast.

On the skeleton knight's horse, she witnessed haunting images that made no sense to her brain. Scattered musical instruments liquefied on jagged cliffs. Piano keys melted. Violin strings dripped. Saxophones pooled around puddles of trombones.

Two angels fought over a stick of gum next to a dying cactus. They wrestled, punched, and even bit at each other's cheeks. Blood oozed all over their wings. Feathers fell, each time they cursed. In the end, the gum tore into tiny pieces of nothing, and the angels collapsed onto the desert ground and wept.

Diana leaned into the skeleton knight's back and whispered, "Why do I feel trepidation sizzle down my spine like an electric charge? Why have I not done what I'm so good at doing—telling the truth?"

"What is the truth? Is he a bad man?"

"I don't know."

"You are Don Quixote," the skeleton knight proclaimed. "You seek justice and chivalry in a world that only has deception."

"I'm only a woman."

"Does that mean you're weak?"

Diana reared back, her face aghast. "Of course not. I've

conquered more things than any male reporter in my industry, and I did it through stealth and determination. I did it with hard work and an all-powering addiction to know the whole story."

They arrived at an old wooden inn. Cracked red paint decorated the front. Stress teased at Diana's temples as she gazed at the foundation that seemed to be softening on the sides. Hard walls melted before her eyes, straighten, hardened, and then liquefied.

The knight jumped off his skinless horse and helped her down. "I know a good man here."

"I think we're going to drown in that building."

"Aren't those the best places to visit, the ones that will consume you?"

Before Diana could answer, someone opened the inn's door.

Asher.

He wore some frilly, white smock. His blonde curls glowed in the light. A black cat sat in Asher's arms. The whole time, the furry animal purred and licked at its paws.

Asher's voice rang out like a song as he extended his hand. "Welcome to my haven."

Diana didn't shake his hand. "Your haven is melting."

"It does that at times."

She looked down at the animal on his arms. "What is the name of your cat?"

Asher grinned. "Diana."

And then the skeleton knight cried out in pain.

Diana turned to her new friend, hoping to help him out.

But it was too late.

Black snakes tore out of his ribcage. His jaw broke apart and dropped to the sandy ground with a boom. The rest of his bones followed. All of them, piece by piece, raining down into a pile. The snakes swarmed around him, slipping and sliding all over the heap of gray bones, gnawing on anything they could get their fangs on.

Diana screamed and ran toward him. "No!"

Asher grabbed her. He must've dropped the cat, but regardless, he trapped her shivering frame into his arms. "Don't cry, Sweet One. Neil was only a skeleton of a man."

She struggled out of his arms and faced him in horror. "What did you say?"

"Neil was only a skeleton of a man."

Screaming and grasping at the covers, Diana woke up in bed.

Asher's bed.

Cupid's bed.

Reality slammed into her chest at once. She was no longer in that weird world of fighting angels and skeleton knights, melting instruments and liquid buildings. No relief swam down on her. In that moment, neither reality nor Diana's dream world appealed to her.

What the hell did that dream mean?

She wiped the sweat off her face, inhaled, exhaled, and fell back into soft pillows.

I know one thing. I'm the cat in Asher's arms, the one licking its paws. I'm such a fucking curious cat.

She scanned the room and made sure he wasn't in there, hovering over her with a bow and arrow.

Where is he? What is he going to do next? What does he want with me?

Her thoughts scattered into jumbled logic and crazed notions.

I'm such a curious cat. It burns in me. Curiosity.

She sat up, picked up the glass of water on her nightstand, and swallowed the warm liquid.

I just had to look in his closet. I just had to be curious. That shitty curiosity sits at the bottom of my gut, and swells with a boiling sludge that never gives me any rest. Over and over, that curiosity churns against my insides. It breathes, at times pushing out my chest, expanding my lungs, and filling me with something more powerful than oxygen.

With both hands, she gripped her head and shook it wildly like a mad woman.

And he burns in me,
Asher,
Cupid.

He burns me so many ways, heating that space between

my earlobe and neck where his breath brushes my skin. He warms the swell of my breast with his fingertips. He sets my pussy on fire, just from moving inside of me.

Arousal hit her core. If she wasn't such a coward, she would touch herself, feel just how wet she could become over a...killer.

What's wrong with me? I want more. But Asher ... Cupid ... is a murderer. Think, Diana. Think.

She'd remembered taking the pills and falling asleep last night. But there were other things she couldn't get out of her head. Right before she'd entered Cupid's last crime scene and read his carved-out message, Asher, the killer himself, had said the most haunting thing to her.

"I hadn't planned on our evening going as it did, but now curiosity trapped the cat, and the cage... it is a big one, a whole island, and you're stuck here, my cat. Don't make me prove it."

Asher leaned her way and landed a kiss onto her shivering forehead. "This isn't to scare you. I just don't want you to do anything stupid, when you walk into the crime scene, witness the gore, and decide that one of those buffoons in uniforms will help you. I'll need you to rethink a foolish escape."

Diana had been about to beg for him to stop talking crazy, "Asher—"

"No, you're not a cat. Curious, yes. But you're not a cat. You're a bird." He brushed his lips against her ear. "Ovid Island and my mansion is all your cage, and you are my bird.

And like a lovely bird, I want to keep you all to myself. Do you have any questions?"

She'd had tons of them, but she couldn't move her lips. Couldn't form words. What more could she have done in that moment?

Back in Cupid's bed, Diana returned to her predicament.

Last night played over and over in her head, banging hard against her skull and delivering a long, continuous ringing sound to her brain. She couldn't think, and though she'd slept, she was still exhausted.

What the hell was my dream telling me? That I'm a mad woman, similar to Don Quixote? And like the crazy man from that story, I've donned an old suit of armor and embarked on a quest to breathe justice back into the world? No.

She closed her legs, her wet pussy smoothing together, those moist folds hugging the desire in. A soft moan fled her lips.

This isn't about justice. This is about sex and my desperate attempt to make this man my hero. I have to stop this, and really figure out the mystery. Vigilante or serial killer?

She sat back.

The men Asher killed weren't innocent. They hurt so many. Was it Asher's place to play God? Was it his place to kill a man who loved raping girls? Was it his place to carve his name so crudely into the flesh like a jeer to the police?

"I'm Cupid—come find me."

I don't shed tears for the men Cupid killed. Not even my

husband. Is the world better off with these men dead?

Sunlight filtered through the bedroom window. She remained in bed, struggling to conjure up justifications for not running away.

She was sure that she'd done the right thing by leaving the crime scene with Asher and returning to his mansion. It would be safer for Diana to be near him and watch her own back, than if she'd fled and always had to glance over her shoulder.

And the truth was that she was more afraid of what lived inside of her. The ribbon of righteousness that drummed through her. No, she couldn't imagine killing for fun. But did she blame Asher for doing what justice should've done?

I'm not a coward, but I'm scared, terrified that my weakening loyalty to the real world is crumbling beneath me. I stood for something. Once. And then Neil happened. And then Asher happened.

And then I realized that I fucked a murderer.

I am insane.

All day she sat there, mumbling and writing deranged sentences in her head. It was like her heart and mind couldn't deal with what had happened in the past weeks—Neil's death, her desperately falling into bed with Asher so quickly in some fast attempt to feel whole again, finding the bow, arrow, and gloves, Asher's confession, and dear God, the message he'd written in blood above his last victim's body.

It was a wonder Diana could even form sentences in her shivering brain.

I can't be Don Quixote. The dream is wrong. Quixote rechristened his horse Rocinante and renamed a peasant woman Dulcinea del Toboso, his queen and lady with hair of gold, and eyebrows like rainbows, cheeks of roses, teeth of pearls, and eyes like suns. He created the reality around him, and truly lived.

She chewed on the end of her hair, realized she was doing it, and then switched to biting her nails.

My life is not a book.

I am not a heroine in a dark romance.

No.

I'm a cat, just as curious. And although the famous proverb states that curiosity killed the cat, I never forget the ending of that same proverb, the one my parents and my society tried to hide. The one nobody wants fellow cats like me to remember.

Curiosity killed the cat, but satisfaction brought it back.

And I have nine lives.

Or do I?

CHAPTER TWO

DIANA

Asher didn't show his face the whole day, never came into the room. She didn't even think he'd slept in the same bed with her last night.

Good.

Hours after she woke and battled with her scattered thoughts, a servant brought breakfast.

Her foot sat on a tray with roses carved into its wooden edges.

So beautiful.

For hours, the toast and sausage sat there untouched. A few flies drew near and landed on the bread. The ice melted in the orange juice, liquid pooling around the glass and wetting the pink cloth napkins. Warm, cheesy scrambled eggs transformed to cold, uneaten bits of flesh on a bone white plate.

She hadn't even picked up the fork, just stared at the butter knife for hours and wondered if anyone would report that it was gone.

Can I sneak it away, without anyone knowing it?

By the afternoon, she remained between the sheets and drowning in anxious thoughts. Her phone vibrated occasionally and she simply ignored them all. How could she possibly talk to someone after the events she'd experienced? How could she be expected to live in the real world when she felt as if she were cascading through a dream?

The servant had already knocked, slipped in, grabbed the breakfast tray, and left another one for lunch. The new food teased at her rumbling and empty stomach—grilled crab legs floating in truffle butter, shrimp risotto topped in shredded fresh parmesan, and a tall glass of lemonade with bits of fruit swimming throughout the sugary liquid.

Right as she gave up on starving herself, she picked up the glass and her phone buzzed.

It made her jump, and she released the lemonade so fast, that it dropped to the ground and spilled all over the ivory carpet.

She didn't bother to saturate the liquid with a towel, instead, she grabbed the phone and checked the text.

Asher: *We're going to a charity event, tonight. Your gown and shoes will be delivered to your door by this evening.*

She wasted no time and typed a reply.

Diana: *What charity event? Why? What time?*

He never responded.

That put her on edge even more.

What was going through his head? He obviously didn't plan to keep her locked up forever, so what *did* he want to do with her? Would he be surprised to learn that if he just talked to her, they might find a common ground?

Her lunch turned cold on her plate. The crab legs looked like cut-up corpses, the splattered lemonade, urine. The risotto appeared more like a small hill of rotting maggots.

Just when Diana thought she might vomit, someone knocked on the door.

Grace entered, and disappointment filled Diana.

What is going through your mind, Asher?

She'd been tired of waiting for what would happen next. If he was going to torture her, then do it. If he had plans for other things, then let them begin. It was the waiting in dark confusion that had her gripping the sheets and sweating.

"What happened?" Grace stepped into the room with a huge white box in both arms.

"What do you mean?" Diana froze.

"Did you spill your drink?" Grace laid the box on the bed and pointed to the lemonade's mess.

"Um, yes." Diana gazed at the walls and wondered if Asher had some sort of spying device in the room. "I spilled the lemonade."

Grace eyed her with curiosity. "Are you okay, Mrs. Carson?"

Will he kill me, if I try to get help from Grace? Jesus.

Would he kill Grace?

"Y-yes. I'm fine." Diana cleared her throat. "What's in the box?"

"I'm not sure. The maids are on their break so I figured I would be nice and take the delivery up to you myself. They're always helping me out in the kitchen."

Diana gave her a tight-lipped smile. "Thank you, Grace."

"When they finish with their break, I'll have them come up and clean this mess."

Diana's voice screeched. "Sounds great."

Grace stared for a second longer. "Are you sure you're okay, Mrs. Carson?"

"Of course."

Grace left, and Diana rushed over to the box and tore it open. Gasping, she lifted the gown out of the tissue paper.

Asher had delivered a piece of fashioned art, draped in crimson pearls.

It was a breathtaking gown, dripping with glamour and sophistication. She was sure it would form around her body in perfection. Each crimson pearl was hand-sewn into the silky fabric. There'd been great care when the person made it.

However, upon gazing at that lovely gown, all Diana could think about was how similar it looked to blood. Like the deep crimson stains splattered across last night's crime scene.

Her phone buzzed again. She placed the gown back into its box and checked the text.

Asher: *Do you like the dress?*

Diana: *Yes, but you never answered my questions.*

Asher: *Be ready by eight o'clock. I'll meet you downstairs.*

Diana: *What charity event is this?*

Asher: *The Monster's Ball.*

Is he serious? Is that a joke or a threat?

The rest of the day lifted her out of depression. She spent hours researching the charity event, which actually *was* The Monster's Ball.

Why is he taking me to this? What's going on?

When the skies darkened and the moon replaced the sun, she dragged her behind out of bed, jumped in the shower, and did her best to gain control of her thoughts.

She'd been doing just fine, until a knock came at the door, and Asher's dark voice sliced through the hard wood. "Diana? It's eight o'clock. Are you ready?"

"I..." She breathed in and out, counted to ten, and breathed in and out some more.

"Diana?" He knocked again and opened the door. "Are you okay?"

She stepped back and stared at him.

Even though there was only dim lighting from her dresser's lamp, she saw every detail of his beauty. Her skin shivered in need. She couldn't help but lick her lips, and taste herself, wishing the whole time that it was him on her tongue, and inside her mouth.

I'm even worse off than I thought. I'm sick.

He wore a beautifully cut tuxedo, one that hugged his body with perfection and displayed that chiseled frame. Those blonde curls were slicked back. The style showed off his gorgeous face and couldn't hide the haunting edge of his jawline, those cheekbones, and full lips. It didn't deafen his exotic allure.

Wicked lust rose within her flesh and disturbed her mind all in the same moment.

"Are you okay?" he asked.

"No. I'm not your bird. I'm a curious cat," she whispered to herself, "And I have nine lives."

"What did you say?" Asher stepped inside the room.

She inched back, nearly tripping over her new red stilettos. "Please, stay right there."

"I told you that I won't hurt you."

"It doesn't mean we need to be next to each other. Please, stay right there."

He obeyed. "I can barely hear you. What did you say?"

"Nothing important."

"Anything that comes out of your mouth is important to me."

"Why?"

He dug his hands into his pockets. "You're my obsession."

And you are mine, Asher.

Diana looked down at her shaking hands. "Obsessions never turn into happy endings."

"Is that what you want, a happy ending?" He asked,

tilting his head to the side.

She turned to the mirror and placed her back to him. "I'll be ready in a few minutes."

He remained there, his reflection only a dark, faceless figure in the mirror.

"Are you not going to answer the question?" he asked.

"What was it?"

"Do you want a happy ending with me?"

"I don't think it's possible." She struggled with putting her new lipstick on. Every time she brought her hand to her mouth, a shiver ran through her body and she got the dark red makeup on her chin.

It looked like drops of blood, and all Diana wanted to do was scream.

"I'll be downstairs." Asher left the room.

And still
those screams
roared
and
scraped
against her skull.

CHAPTER THREE

ASHER

Maxwell Grayson was a jackass,
and
Asher's next victim.

Maxwell had a thing for Halloween. He firmly believed ghouls and ghosts should be celebrated all year long.

In a way, Asher agreed. Cupid was a monster, a ghoul, a ghost weaving in and out of people's lives to fix what was broken. He most certainly should be celebrated all year long.

Maxwell held charity events almost every month for his foster home and themed each party. His Witches' Brew was in November on his large estates, where artisan-brewing companies flew in to provide their new beers for tasting and auctioning. On the south end of Ovid Island in December, he threw a gala called Santa's Haunted Pole. Nude women painted in green and red strolled the event with bruised faces and fake scars all over their arms. In their hands, they held paintings for sale by local artists.

All the money went to his foster kids.

In January, Maxwell hosted the Monster's Ball at Ovid Island's art museum. The tickets cost close to a thousand to attend, and Asher never saw the point of it all. People just got dressed up in gowns and suits to watch others, poorer people from Miami's mainland, prance around in horror costumes.

Again, all the money went to Maxwell's large foster home.

Yet,
it's been said that Maxwell went to his foster home too,
late at night,
when everyone was asleep,
and he did unholy things to his favorite kids, boys and girls, the ones that so many people had tossed money to him to save.

He'd look at his partygoers and tell them how much he *loved* the kids, and the unsuspecting fools had no idea just how *much* he loved them. How much he loved to make them cry and scream and beg to be let go of.

Maxwell was a son of a bitch, and Asher would kill him, pull back his bow, target his arrow's point, and then release.

The only problem was when.

Not how, but when he had the time.

It was just Maxwell's bad luck that he delivered an invitation to Asher on that day, the morning after Diana discovered that he was Cupid. The morning after his pounding headache and huge argument with his dead mother's ghost. He'd been ready to put his arrow in somebody, and Maxwell served as the perfect target.

That he would go to this Monster's Ball wasn't even a question. The event provided a perfect opportunity to get close to the sicko, learn his daily habits, get a good look at the man's property, find the weak spots, and come up with an efficient way to kill.

Diana would have to come too. He couldn't leave his bird in her cage. Sometimes the bird keeper had to let the creature out, get her away from the cold bars, and let her wings spread and her feathers ruffle in the wind.

On the invitation, Maxwell requested that the men wear tuxedos and all the women should dress in gowns the color of blood. Asher had reread the line over and over, unsure if he was hallucinating.

Diana dressed in blood?

The very thought triggered a dark lust to shiver through him. His cock hardened right there in his pants. An urge swelled in him. He wanted to race to his bedroom, take Diana's small frame onto his bed, and slip inside of her,

in and out,

until day turned to night,

and her memories of meeting Cupid disappeared.

I can't. She'll never let me touch her again. I could see it in her eyes, last night. She's never going to stop being afraid of me.

The rest of the day, he forced himself to focus on the Ball

and all the things he had to do—get Diana's gown, jewelry, and shoes, notify the staff of his absence, and find out if Maxwell would be at his event.

Hours later, night came to the land.

Ovid Island was south of Miami's coastline. A paradise for the filthy rich. A getaway for lonely souls looking to get into trouble.

But lately with all the murders of wealthy men, people no longer declared that Ovid Island was paradise. Even the setting changed overnight, as if the island itself, breathed on its own and had become sick from all of the spilled blood and violence.

The glowing moon sat in a sky where no stars sparkled. The palm trees appeared less glorious, and more like bushy skeletal bodies that slanted side to side in the wind.

A horrid smell rode the night breeze.

During the day, storm clouds hovered and cold streets met violent tires that zoomed past. Rich men didn't cruise along the island anymore in their expensive cars, ogling curvy women that bounced around in tennis outfits. Now, men sped by fast and rushed to the safety of their homes, encased with security alarms and a hungry Rottweiler, as if alarms and dogs could keep them safe from Cupid.

There'd been some sort of yacht accident on the southern tip of Ovid Island—two drunk billionaires crashed into each other.

Two dumbass alcoholics with too much time and money, didn't look where they were driving and smashed their yachts into each other. The news had been all over the island, due to one of the men having their mistress with them—she'd broken his arm, he'd ruined his marriage.

Asher wished Cupid could take credit but alas – it was their own stupidity that led to their injuries and deaths. Not the righteous justification of a bow and arrow.

After the accident, a disgusting odor drenched the land. Fluids leaked from the yachts and poured into the sea. The watery surface around the island now shined oily black and bubbled in some places. Dead fish washed up under the piers.

Residents complained. Some argued about the smell. The police dropped the investigation of Cupid's latest victim, and dealt with the accident.

Maxwell should've canceled the ball. Not many people will come tonight. The men are scared they'll die. The women won't be able to smell their designer perfume over the gassy odor.

Asher's driver made sure to keep the limo windows up, as Diana and Asher rode in the back and headed to the Ball.

"Have you ever been to Maxwell's charity events?" Asher asked.

Dressed in sparkling blood, Diana shook her head no and remained quiet.

When she'd finally walked downstairs, Asher had clenched his teeth and almost locked his damn jaw, trying to keep the groan inside of his mouth from escaping. The crimson pearls brought out the rich chocolate of her flesh, made him want to take a lick, a long lap with his tongue.

And those lovely breasts pushed against the top of her gown and bounced with each step.

Fuck yes.

If he'd truly been a monster, he would've charged at her, clasped his hands on her body, ripped away every shiny pearl and silky inch of fabric, and exposed those lush pillows to the world.

This was a bad idea. I shouldn't have invited her to the ball. I'll never focus on what I need to.

He craved just one tug,
just one long wet tug of his mouth on one of her nipples,
she could choose which one.

His cock begged and throbbed in his pants.

His heart pounded in his chest.

Blood rushed to everywhere, but his brain.

All he hungered for was just one lovely tug, one never-ending session of sucking on any nipple that she'd let him feast on.

In that captivating gown, she had stopped at the stairs, looked up at him, and widened her eyes. "Is something wrong?"

All he could do was grunt and point to the front door. Diana had been smart to give him space as she stepped by him. If she only knew the things that played in his mind—like her nude flesh drenched in blood and sex.

It took him longer than normal to meet her in the limo. He'd waited in that hallway for a few minutes, just for his erection to go down and his mind to clear of the demented fog of desire.

When he got into the car, she turned his way. "Are you sure you're okay?"

"Yes."

"Fine." Although the limo's shadows hid most of her face, a little light bounced around the ruby teardrops that dangled from her ears. He'd spent all morning searching for the perfect pair of earrings to go with that gown.

Perhaps, I made her too perfect this evening.

He gripped the edge of his seat and asked her again, "Have you ever been to Maxwell's charity events?"

"No."

"Why not?"

"I wasn't allowed to. Neil thought it was better for me to be seen at only the important events. It wasn't worth it to argue with him. I'd never heard anything but gossip about the parties anyway. I wouldn't have enjoyed myself and watching Neil... play games."

At the mention of her husband's name, his body tensed. "Are you mad that I killed Neil and his mistress?"

She parted her lips and didn't respond.

She's on edge tonight.

Well, of course she is. I murdered her husband and now

I've basically kidnapped her. What should she be doing, laughing and making jokes? Damn it. What have I done? This is all out of control. Did I just ask her if she was mad I killed her husband? Of course she is.

Diana's soft voice disrupted his thoughts. "You're twisting the end of your tuxedo jacket into a knot."

"What?" He snapped his attention to her. "I'm doing what?"

"You're mumbling incoherent words and twisting your jacket."

He looked down and sure enough, violent wrinkles covered the right side of his tuxedo. "Sorry."

She turned her gaze to the window next to her. "There's nothing to be sorry about."

"No?"

"No."

He swallowed and slumped into his seat. "That can't be right. I'm sure I have a lot to apologize for."

Silence.

Quiet prevailed. It slithered between them and thickened the air molecules to sludgy unbreathable things.

Asher pressed the window's button. The glass slid down. A breeze spilled in and cooled his skin. And then that horrid odor from the yachting accident rushed inside—dead fish rotting in an oily ocean.

"Damn it." He put the window back up, realized he cursed, and said, "Sorry."

"It's fine."

"I'm on edge," he explained.

"It's fine."

"How are you, Diana?"

"I'm fine."

"And are you—"

"Fine," she said. "Everything is fine."

He groaned and rubbed his face with his hands. "Stop it."

"Stop what?" She faced him.

"You know what you're doing?"

She tossed him a mocking pout. "What am I doing, sir?"

That *sir* stabbed at his insides. A word like that didn't belong on her lips. Diana was a beast, too strong to bow down to any man and refer to him as her equal.

"Stop it," he said through clenched teeth.

"Stop what?" She raised her eyebrows. "Stop being an obedient prisoner? Stop sitting in the limo? Stop talking to you? Stop shaking underneath my gown? Stop praying inside of my head that you won't hurt me? Stop wondering if I'm going to turn into someone I never thought I'd be, a scared animal trapped in a cage? Are these the things that you want me to stop?"

Shocked, he whispered, "Yes."

The swell of her breasts rose as she breathed in and then exhaled. "Would you rather I try to run? Do you want to chase me, before you take my life? Is that the whole plan? Are you into the psychological part, even more than the copper scent of blood and the ragged tearing of flesh? Stop what exactly? Tell me old bird keeper, because my mind is intrigued. Stop being a bird? Do you want me to be a cat? Or should I be Don Quixote?"

"Don Quixote?" Asher began twisting his jacket again. "What does this have to do with Don Quixote?"

"Stop what exactly?"

He opened his mouth and just stared.

She pointed at him. "You fucking scare me."

Asher inched away and leaned against his side of the limo, his back pressing into the window. He assumed that he had frightened her, but in what way? She was making jokes on her life, toying with him. It was clear she was scared... but of which part of him?

"Look at this." She extended her hands in front of her and showed him those shaking fingers. "That is my brain."

"Your hands are your brain?"

"No!" she yelled.

Asher jumped, but doubted she noticed.

"My shaking is the sign that I have a brain."

"Of course you do."

She sighed. "You don't even know what I'm talking about. You just think that I'm hysterical or something."

You're definitely hysterical. I hadn't realized how much I scared you.

"I'm sorry, Diana."

"I'm not going crazy," she argued.

"I don't really think that I'm a good person to judge if you're crazy or not." He risked a shrug. "But you did just mention Don Quixote."

"Because it is all related!"

"Okay." He nodded. "Then am I Don Quixote?"

"No." She buried her face into her hands. "I am."

"Then I'm Sancho? That was his friend, right? A farmer."

"Oh just forget about it. That doesn't matter."

"I think it does. Are you saying that my kills are like a farmer, am I growing—"

"Just stop it. You've missed the point." She blew out a long breath. "I'm Don Quixote and am walking around in a surreal world. You're not Sancho. You're Dulcinea."

He scrunched his face up in disgust. "The female that Don Quixote loved?"

"Would you just forget about me saying Don Quixote? That's not the problem."

"I don't know. You just said I was a poor waitress."

"She was a peasant woman."

"That's no better."

"Why because she's a peasant or the fact that she's a woman?"

He waited a few seconds before responding, "I don't think I should answer that."

She stared at him. "Why not?"

"Because it might get me in further trouble with you."

"Further trouble? That ship has sailed, buddy." She shook her head in disbelief. "You've kidnapped me. I'm in your home against my will. You've admitted to being a murderer. A serial killer."

"I never said that I was a serial killer."

She pointed that accusing finger at him some more. "You never denied it."

"You never asked."

"I shouldn't have to."

"I don't hurt anyone that doesn't deserved to be destroyed."

The next words left her mouth in a shriek. "YOU ARE NOT GOD!"

"What does this all have to do with Don Quixote?"

"Would you just forget about that?!"

Asher was sure his driver had caught some of her yelling. He'd had the divider up the whole time between the driver and them, yet classical music soared from the front of the limo as if the driver had turned it up to block the conversation.

"Please, keep your voice down." Asher sighed. "Mother used to scream at me in the back of here. Now that she's gone, I'm not going to deal with it anymore."

Her voice came out shaky. "What would you do to me, if I kept on screaming like your mother?"

He shook his head. "I would just ask you to be quiet again, and hope you would listen."

She formed her lips into a straight line.

"I'm not a monster all of the time, Diana." He directed his attention to the window. "Just on days that end with y."

"You scare me."

He closed his eyes. "Yeah. Well, you scare me too."

"I-I won't tell—"

"You will. You can't help it. You'll tell my story. I think I just figured that out last night as I lay in bed and wondered why I didn't kill you... "

He didn't have to open his eyes and turn to know that her muscles had gone rigid. That his admission had either confirmed her fears or brought about new ones. Regardless, he had to lay it all on the line. Start telling the truth. If only so that she could get ahold of her mind and realize that she was safe with him... at least for now.

"Why didn't you kill me?"

"I don't have it in me to hurt you, Diana." That time he did open his eyes and face her. But instead of remaining calm, he moved all the way to her side of the limo so that barely a few inches remained between them.

What went on in her mind, with them being so close?

He inhaled the scent of lush roses. That beautiful fragrance radiated from her skin. His body warmed. Was she as hot as him? Or had she frozen into icy fear?

"I murder people who hurt others. I take their lives because they injured innocent people. I don't just go around shooting my arrow at anybody. You think I'm a serial killer?"

"I-I don't know what you are."

"I'm the guy that does what the police should."

"Are you a vigilante?"

"No, I'm Cupid."

"That's not an answer."

"Think, Diana. You know the history of my so-called victims. Do you fit their descriptions?" He leaned in closer.

Three inches sat between the tips of their noses.

"No." She sank into her side and moved away from him. "That doesn't mean I'm safe."

"No, it doesn't mean you're safe. You're the first woman that's ever stirred up these weird emotions inside of me. I should've killed you, when you discovered my bow and arrow, but I didn't."

"How did you know I found it?"

"I have cameras in all of the rooms."

She gasped. "You watched me?"

"I've been watching you for a while."

So close. They were so close to each other, but neither moved away.

"You're not safe," he whispered.

Inhaling Diana some more, Asher closed the tiny space between them and brushed his lips against hers. She shivered under his mouth, and he had no idea if it was from lust or disgust.

But her breathing shifted to a steady rhythm as her chest slowly rose and fell. The flesh on her neck looked ready to bite. And she hadn't turned away from his mouth or shut her eyes or cried out for help or anything that would make him reel back to his side of the limo and cease his mouth's probing.

"You're not safe, Diana." He licked his lips and battled with himself to not release his stiff cock that grew even harder in his pants. "Do you want me to move?"

A tear spilled from her eye. "No. I should."

He nipped her bottom lip. "Yes, you should."

Her voice came out as some ragged plea. "Why can't I?"

"I don't know. I'm just as addicted to you, as you are to me. We're both going to be our demise. You know that right?"

"You're scaring me."

"I'm scaring myself." He devoured her mouth. Their lips smoothed against each other and made wet slurping sounds.

It was madness. Flames ignited, and there was no turning back. He couldn't stop himself anymore. She'd been so hurt, so weak and scared as she talked in the limo, and all he could think of was wrapping his arms around her quaking frame and holding her the rest of the night.

Once the kissing started, his thoughts changed.

He imagined the tip of his hungry length outlining her moist center. He'd play with those secret lips first, open and close them slowly with his wicked fingers, see how much she would wriggle in her seat and beg for him to part those folds and fuck her hard until her mind exploded.

"I'm going to do something," he mumbled between wet kisses. "And I don't want you to be scared."

The words that fled her mouth were caught between short exhales as if she'd been running and couldn't calm her breathing. "What are you going to do?"

"I'm going to tear your dress apart." He reached for her breasts and clutched them in his huge hands. "I've wanted these in my mouth since the moment you walked down those stairs."

She moved his hands away.

His next words were growls. "Don't do that."

"Do what?" She still held his hand away from her breasts. "You can't just rip my gown. We're going to the ball, and I don't even know if..."

"What?"

"If I can have sex with you."

He gritted his teeth. "Okay."

"Do you understand?"

He didn't respond; too busy attempting to water down the fire that roared in his bones.

"Why are we going to the ball anyway?" she asked.

"I don't want to talk about the ball right now. I want you."

"Asher, why are we going to this ball?"

He moved in to nip at her neck.

She ducked and shoved at him. "Stop it."

He backed up and returned to his side of the limo, but not before emitting an odd growling sound. What had occurred? They'd entered the vehicle with tension and fear mingling in the air. And now, sex merged with blinding desire, and the whole time Diana held his puppet strings.

Does she even realize how much power she has over me? What's going to happen to us?

"Why are we going to this Ball?" she asked again.

"Why do you think there has to be a reason?"

"Because, you want me there."

"I didn't want to leave you by yourself, so you could do more snooping."

"You're lying. I've already discovered your secret. What else could I possibly find? So, tell me, why are we really going?"

He stared at her with amused eyes. She was adorable for thinking she knew all there was to know about him. He decided not to push it and tell the truth instead. "Maxwell is going to be my next victim."

"Why?"

"Because he likes to hurt foster boys and girls."

"How?"

"There's no need to discuss the details."

"Tell me."

He shifted in his seat. "Why, so that you can feel better about this?"

"No, so I can understand," she corrected. "How did you even find out he hurt his foster kids? Where do you get your intel?"

"It's not intel. I start with gut feelings. Two months ago, there'd been reports around the island about how he'd fired his private nurse that served at the foster home. People wondered why. As did I." He turned away from her. "Any gossip dealing with kids intrigues me."

"Why?"

"Because kids need protection. They're young and weak, and subservient to whoever resides within the four walls of their home."

"O-kay."

"Maxwell had handed the foster home's nurse a huge

amount of money and sent her far off. I got to her, before she was due to leave the island."

"What do you mean, got to her?"

"I came to her late in the night, sat on her bed in the darkness with my hood on, woke her up, and simply asked what had happened."

"You scared the shit out of her."

"Doesn't matter."

"It does. You can't just—"

"Twelve cases of syphilis."

Diana paused. "What?"

"The nurse had discovered twelve cases of syphilis in the kids at the foster home, and they were all under ten years old. Add the fact that she'd just treated Maxwell for syphilis over six months ago, and it didn't take her long to put two and two together."

"Jesus."

"Jesus didn't save those kids."

"Don't say that."

He put his back to her. "It's true. Jesus didn't come down and save them."

"So you're Jesus?"

"No, but I think I was put here by God for another purpose. Everyone has a purpose in life. I think death is mine."

"So now you're the grim reaper?"

"No, I'm Cupid apparently."

Quiet passed and then Diana broke the silence. "Did you

kill the nurse?"

"No, why would I do that?"

"She took the money and left, knowing that the kids were in trouble."

"No, she'd planned on putting in an anonymous complaint, and praying that it stopped him. What else could she do? Maxwell is a powerful man. In this country, that's enough to get away with murder." He grinned. "It's why I reside in America."

Diana shivered as if a chill ran through her. "How long has it been since you talked to the nurse?"

"Months ago. I'm sure Maxwell has done more. It's been hard to come up with a good plan, when so many others should die—"

"Maxwell should've died before Neil, at least. If this is true."

"Interesting." He laughed. "I don't prioritize my kills like I should. I just go for the easy ones first. Neil provided no problem. He was too busy playing mind games with you and fucking everyone around town."

She frowned and looked away.

"But, now I'm coming for Maxwell."

"You don't know if the nurse actually told the truth. She could've been a disgruntled employee. Maybe *she* gave them syphilis, and he fired her, but gave her money so the news wouldn't spread and ruin his foundation."

He reached his hand out to her face, touched her chin, and guided her view to him. "Well, that's your job. You're the investigator. I keep Maxwell busy. You look around."

"The art museum?" she asked.

"No, the foster home. It's right next to the museum where the Ball is being held. Do what you do best. Dig."

She flinched at the last word and muttered, "Maybe, I'll just run off and escape."

He laughed and gripped her chin tighter than he should have. "No, Diana. Trust me. You want to walk side by side with me while I hunt. Not be the one that I'm looking for in the shadows."

CHAPTER FOUR

DIANA

Diana's heels clicked against the pavement as Asher guided her toward Ovid Island's Art Museum.

"Are you cold?" Asher asked.

"No."

He turned around without saying anything more. Though it had only been a twenty-minute car ride to the museum, it had felt like hours. Thick tension spread between them like molasses. Desire bubbled up from the pit of her stomach and mixed with disgust that she could still have those feelings for him.

She was dressed in a beautiful gown, on the arm of a beautiful man and yet she felt the world's ugliness bow at her feet. Never in all of her life had Diana experienced such conflicting emotions.

Did she hate Asher? Or revere him? Was she frightened of him? Or frightened of what he could bring out in her?

They entered the Monster's Ball, and the décor fit her mood.

Death and lust.

Hundreds of black skulls hung from the ceiling by gold rope. All their eyes glowed to light the Monster's ball. At least five candles stood in the center of all the many tables. Melted wax dripped onto the table and hardened around all of them, setting the gloom of the room even further.

The room was so dark, she didn't get a clear view of everyone's faces, just shadowed light over naked skin. Giggles rode the music and merged with the clatter of forks hitting dishes.

Long mirrors decorated the walls.

They walked past one, and she realized that they weren't mirrors at all. Ghostly nude images danced on their glass surface and waved back at them. Some opened their mouths and released silent shrieks as they pinched their nipples. Others floated in the center of the frame, stroking their long cocks, their eyes distant as if death had blinded them.

Waiters carried monstrous things on plates. Diana peered at one and tensed. A tiny, burnt face greeted her eyes. It lay there on the plate, some sort of meat formed into a blackened head with garlic as the fangs, olives for the eyes, and a red sauce smearing it into a bloody effect.

Asher tilted his head her way as they took their time moving further into the ballroom. "Are you hungry?"

Her stomach rumbled, but he probably couldn't hear it.

"No. I'm fine."

"Not that again."

"I *am* fine."

"And you're Don Quixote too, apparently."

"Would you leave that alone?"

He smirked. "I really wish I could, but now I'll probably go dig up a copy and read the story again. I bet there's one in my library."

"Where's Maxwell?" She tried to let go of his hand.

He wouldn't release it. "Don't worry. He'll come to us."

She gave up with pulling her hand away. "How do you know that?"

"Because I sent him a message that I want to donate a million dollars to his foundation. That should get me some extra ass kissing time during the ball."

She nodded. "He's probably been searching for you all night."

"Definitely." He led her onto the dance floor. "Let's cut through here."

She focused on the music as she followed behind him.

A band performed on the stage far in the back. Haunting make-up covered the musicians' faces. An ax sat in the lead singer's head as he strummed his guitar and sang in a slow rhythm, *"When the moon bleeds, I'll come to you. I'll save you. I'll conquer you."*

The singer's voice twisted Diana's heart, so low and sad, yet full of malice and lust too.

"When the moon bleeds, I'll find you. I'll capture the very thing that makes you."

Asher squeezed her hand as he led her further into the sea of elegant people. Ovid's finest crowded the hall, although less of a number than most events. Jewels glittered in the soft light. Red shined and glimmered on every woman. Some wore gloves. Almost everyone dripped in rubies. A few donned tiaras and chokers that Diana knew cost a fortune.

Still, the singer's words helped Diana's walk with her murderous escort.

"You're my possession!" The singer raised his voice almost into a melodious scream. *"I own you! I own you!"*

The drums came in as a guitar followed the singer's chorus.

"There's not a second! That I don't know you! I own you!"

The singer gasped and turned his attention to his guitar and played the notes that words couldn't truly capture. The music grew into a chain and bound around her heart. It somehow entered Diana, not through her ears, but right at the center of her chest, just like she was sure Asher's arrows did to his victims. The band played on. It was haunting.

The notes pierced her, made her pause in the middle of the dance floor and unable to move. Asher stopped with her, turned around, and studied Diana's face in the skull's glowing light.

"When the moon bleeds," the singer began to lower each word to a whispering hum. *"When the moon bleeds."*

Instead of asking her if she was okay, Asher pulled Diana into his arms and guided her body into a sway that moved with the song's rhythm.

"When the moon bleeds."

More dancing people surrounded them. One couple bumped into Asher's elbow. He grimaced at them. They simply giggled in drunken hysteria and twirled away.

"When the moon bleeds."

Asher brushed his lips against Diana's ear. "You're like this song. You make me want to stop and dance. Stop everything and look at life."

She shivered in his arms, yet her body molded against his as they danced. Her nipples hardened in the gown, or maybe they had never softened since the limo ride and Asher's lips. His cologne caged her further, drew her in like one would tease a mouse with cheese.

"You're probably the only thing that could stop me." He sucked on her ear lobe, nibbled a little at the tip. She could've sworn he inhaled her, but it had to be all in her head. Still, she clutched his shoulders, not sure if she could hold onto him anymore.

Is this all really happening or am I in another dream? Why do I want him so much, even when we're surrounded by horror?

And then the song rushed back into hysteria. The drums shifted from a gentle tap to a thunderous boom. The guitar fell into an assault of harmony and lust.

"You're my possession!" the singer screamed. *"I own you! I own you!"*

"Yes." Asher buried his face into the curve of her neck and sucked on her flesh as if he was a vampire, preparing a woman for the sharp edge of his fangs. She let her head fall back, allowed this man, this killer to feast on her skin, just for the simple fact that it felt so damn good. Her pussy ached for his lips to explore it the same way they he feasted on her neck.

She remembered how skilled he was between her thighs. He'd tasted her like there was nothing else on the planet that could feed him.

"There's not a second! That I don't own you! I own you! I own you!"

She closed her eyes, shook against him, and had no idea if it was fear, the music, or Asher causing it all.

"I!" the singer roared into the microphone like a deranged lover. *"I!"*

That dream world swam into her head—skeletons riding on horses, angels wrestling, a rainbow plastered in darkness, and violins melting on a shadowed landscape.

"I! I! I!"

She gasped, pushed away from Asher, and rushed off, stumbling around happy couples and bumping into waiters. She could hardly breathe. Something corroded her lungs. It sat like bricks in her chest, unable to move. She scanned the space and hoped for an exit or a bathroom, somewhere to escape, if only for a few minutes.

I can't let him touch me anymore. I have to stop that.

The drums and guitar went berserk.

I just can't.

The stilettos slowed her down. She limped forward and ignored the ache in her soles. Adrenaline surged through her.

Her heart boomed, until she couldn't hear the music anymore, just the sounds of her own heart beating.

She didn't even glance behind her to see if Asher followed. She knew he would.

"I own you!"

Near the edge of the dance floor, a door opened on her right. Two laughing women in red strolled out. She pushed past them.

"Isn't that Diana Carson," one of them said.

"Haven't seen much from her," the other replied.

"Wasn't her husband one of the ones... you know?"

"Yes."

She ignored them and entered, didn't even turn back to see which one of the high society wenches had spoken her name. The door closed behind her. She locked herself into the private bathroom.

The two women must've been taking turns in the mirror as they freshened up their makeup. Violet and pink powder dotted the edges.

Diana searched the small bathroom for another exit or a window or two. Nothing. Just white solid walls.

Too bad they aren't melting like in my dream.

She slumped against the door.

Where would I have gone anyway? What am I doing now? I'm going to have to face this shit. Whatever I've gotten myself into. I'm going to have to deal with it. What had Asher said, while we danced?

On cue, his voice slipped into her head. "Only you could

stop me."

"Then, that's what I'll do." Diana stumbled toward the toilet and vomited.

CHAPTER FIVE

ASHER

When Diana opened the bathroom door and spotted Asher, terror glazed over her eyes.

She's afraid again? Why?

She dabbed at the corner of her lips with a folded piece of paper towel, and then dropped the crumpled paper into the trashcan that had been decorated like a howling werewolf.

"Are you okay?" he asked.

She shrugged, her rubies dangling at her ears. "No. I'm not okay."

This is never going to work. What am I going to do?

"Do you want this?" He held up a wine glass with dark red liquid. It bubbled at the rim. A cinnamon scented steam rose from its watery surface. "The bartender called it Dracula's Blood."

She forced herself to smile back at him. He could tell it was forced by the way her cheeks shivered as they strained to keep her face in that expression. "And will it give me immortality?"

"You want to live forever?" he asked.

"Right now, I just want to live."

"You will as much as I can control it. I'll always protect you."

"But, Asher, can you protect me from you?"

"I could try."

"That doesn't comfort me."

"What other choice do you have?" He gave her the glass.

"I have plenty of options. Several, in fact." She took the glass to her mouth and drank, tipping the bottom high to finish it all.

When she returned the empty wine glass to him, he frowned and stared at it. "You're thirsty?"

"No, I'm in desperate need to get drunk."

"I don't think that's—"

"Bishop, the wonderful man of the hour!" The voice came from behind them.

Both Asher and Diana turned.

A thin, wiry man with Buddy Holly glasses and a crooked smile faced them.

Maxwell.

When Asher had asked around about Maxwell, everyone always had great things to say about him.

"He's a kid at heart, that Maxwell."

"Such a clown."

"What a lovable character!"

"He just has a way with kids. Always coming by the playground with ice cream and balloons for my twins."

If people didn't brag about his sense of humor or charm, then they celebrated his toy corporation. His family had started in the business over fifty years ago. They'd been one of the first business to see the money in buying gifts for kids. They triggered the craze for certain products through their guerilla advertising around cartoon hour and on sugar coated cereal boxes.

When Maxwell graduated from Princeton and became CEO of Toymania, he took the company even further. The corporation developed a new product line for babies. He'd also come out with an ice cream brand. Each package displayed some of their top-selling toys. Rainbow popsicles inspired kids to yearn for Toymania multicolored building blocks. There were even chocolate dipped cones shaped like action figures and dolls.

"That Maxwell. He sure is a fine guy. He's trying to be a sort of real life Willy Wonka. I heard he's building another factory in India."

Asher gave Maxwell a strained smile and nod. "Ah, I suspected you'd find me at some point."

Maxwell laughed, his glasses shaking slightly as his head bobbed. "Of course, old chap," he winked and then added, "and who is this goddess on your arm?"

Asher cleared his throat. "Diana Carson."

"Pleasure to meet you." Maxwell did a dramatic bow, straightened, and produced a bouquet of roses out of nowhere. At first, Asher had only saw Maxwell's empty fingers. Next, a dozen roses bloomed in front of Diana.

A giggle left her lips. "That's amazing. How did you do that?"

Asher formed his hands into closed fists. "Yes, how *did* you do that?"

"Magic." Maxwell snapped his fingers. A cigar appeared where nothing had been. "Do you like cigars, Asher?"

"That's Mr. Bishop to you, and no I do not."

"You want me to call you Mr. Bishop?" Maxwell chuckled and turned to Diana. "Is he serious?"

Careful, Maxwell. You do not talk to her. I'd planned to give you another night to breathe. That may not happen.

Diana eyed Asher. "I'm not sure, if Asher is serious or not. But, he does love to joke around."

Maxwell hit Asher on the back. "Oh I love a good joker!"

Asher grunted.

"Do you know any good jokes?" Maxwell tucked the cigar in his pocket. "I would love to hear one."

Diana grabbed another glass of Dracula's blood from a server passing by with a full tray. "Yes, Asher or rather, Mr. Bishop. Why don't you tell us one of your hilarious jokes?"

"I only know one." Asher tried to maintain his calm, even after Maxwell got closer to Diana, winked, and nudged her side with his. He stiffened, not used to seeing Diana next to another man. They'd barely known each other themselves, but still, jealousy pricked at his skin.

I don't think straight when she's around.

"Tell us the joke, Mr. Bishop." Diana sipped her second glass.

"Okay. Here it goes," Asher said. "How do you stop a rich man from drowning?"

A wrinkle came on Maxwell's forehead. "Hmmm. I don't know. How *do* you stop a rich man from drowning?"

Asher beamed. "You shoot him in the chest, before he hits the water."

Diana spit out some of her drink and coughed. Of course, Maxwell produced a handkerchief from somewhere and cleaned the few drops off her neck and the top part of her cleavage.

However, both Diana and Maxwell paused as they realized that in the moments of the coughing and cleaning, Asher had come close to them.

Very close.

His huge body dominated their space. "Please, stop touching her."

Maxwell inched back. "Um... I hope I was... helpful."

"You were," Diana replied in annoyance. "My Asher is just a little possessive at times."

Asher grunted and continued to stare at Maxwell. It was hard for him to describe the feeling that overcame his every cell. It had been more than jealousy. Maybe, it was rage. Hot boiling rage.

Besides his mother, he'd never put another woman above himself. Letting Diana live, after she knew that he was a killer, was the only other time he'd allowed another to have something over him.

It made him fragile, as thin and weak as eggshells. And

even though Maxwell probably had no interest in a woman Diana's age, Asher couldn't deal with the man so close to her, his pedophilic fingers touching the tops of her breasts.

You may die tonight, Mr. Wonka.

"I'm sorry." Maxwell raised his hands in the air in mock surrender. "I only meant to help her out."

"Of course." Asher didn't move and continued to tower over him. "Did you like my joke?"

Maxwell backed up some more. "I did. It's rather fitting, being that so many rich men have... you know... "

"Died." Asher widened his mouth into a huge smile.

Diana cleared her throat and hooked her arm around Asher's. "So, your charity really intrigues me, Maxwell. I would love to help."

"It does?" Maxwell raised his bushy eyebrows. "Now... I must confess something. I know who Mr. Bishop is, but I don't know much about you, Mrs. Carson. What do you do?"

Asher pulled her closer. "She's a reporter for the Ovid Island Newspaper and also my date for the evening."

"Carson? That name sounds rather familiar," Maxwell said, scrunching his eyebrows together.

"Perhaps it's because my husband and his mistress were slaughtered by a serial killer last week. By Cupid, to be specific." Diana's smile left her face. "Mr. Bishop has made it his duty to comfort me in my time of need."

"Right, right. I'm so sorry for your loss, Mrs. Carson," Maxwell said. "It must be extremely difficult to deal with this situation."

"You have no idea," Diana mumbled.

Maxwell shifted his weight and studied both of them, his attention going to Diana and then Asher. "I should let you two return to your celebration. However, Mr. Bishop, we should really talk. Your donation." He made an excited face. "That's going to be a big help. You know Thompson's cereal company is matching the total of tonight's donations, so your million dollars will end up being a double contribution."

"I have not made it yet," Asher said. "Like I've told your office, I want to see the foster home."

Maxwell frowned. "You want to see it tonight?"

"Only if you want me to give you my million dollars tonight. If not, then we can schedule a later date."

"No. No. Tonight is fine." Maxwell dug his hands into his pockets and pulled out his phone. "Let me just get my assistant to take you over there. It's right next door, she can give you the tour, while—"

"No," Asher said. "I would like *you* to show me."

"I'm hosting the ball." Maxwell gestured to the packed dance floor and went back to typing into his phone.

"I would like the man behind the foster home to take me on a tour." Asher glanced at Diana. "Sweetheart, you won't mind, if I go off with Maxwell for a few minutes. Right?"

"You want me to stay here?" Shock fell on Diana's face.

"Yes." He leaned in, kissed her cheek, and then whispered in her ear, "Follow us. Stay several feet behind. When he opens the door, I'll make sure you are able to get in. Then do what you do."

Asher let go of her arm and stood back from her. "Okay, Maxwell. Let's go."

Maxwell looked up from his phone. "Are you serious?"

"As serious as a heart attack." Asher laughed. "Hey, that's sort of a joke right there. Heart attacks are funny, right?"

Diana shook her head. "We really need to work on your sense of humor."

"Is it my timing?" Asher quirked his blonde eyebrows.

"I think you're just a little too dark," she said.

Frowning, Maxwell put his phone up. "Yes, I agree." He checked his watch. "Okay, I guess I have a few minutes to show you around. We'll have to be quick. The auction starts in an hour."

"We'll be quick."

"Let me just notify my assistant." Maxwell rushed off. "For some reason, I'm not getting a good signal in the ball room."

As soon as he scurried away, Diana glared at Asher. "Why were you acting so weird?"

"How did he know you loved roses?"

"What?" She handed the bouquet over to him. "Most women like roses. It's a pretty safe pick. And it's a simple magic trick that anyone can do."

A waitress came by. "Would you like another drink, Ma'am?"

"Yes." Diana finished her second one, and grabbed the third.

"And how about you, sir?" The server looked at Asher.

"No, thank you, but could you take these." Asher gave the bouquet to her. "Lovely flowers for a lovely woman."

A blush spread over her face. "Why thank you."

Diana snorted as the waitress winked at him and sashayed away. "You're such a flirt."

"That's not me flirting. That was me simply being nice. You've seen how I flirt." He licked his lips. "Should I remind you?"

"No." She gulped the Dracula's Blood down.

He took the glass from her. "I think you may have had enough."

"I think, I'm a grown ass woman and can decide when I've had enough on my own." She signaled for another server to come.

"How are you going to investigate Maxwell, if you're drunk?"

"Are you serious?"

"I am."

"You don't want me to investigate." She poked at his chest. "You just want me to have busy work."

"No, I want you to understand me."

"I do." She picked up her fourth glass from another waitress, waited for the woman to leave, and declared, "You are a killer."

"Be careful, Diana."

"Even if Maxwell was innocent, you would still make up your mind that he had to die."

"That's not true," he said through clenched teeth. "I

would leave him alone."

"Has that ever happened?"

"No."

"Then you're full of shit." She sipped her drink. "I bet some of your victims were innocent."

"They were."

She blinked twice. "Excuse me?"

He grabbed the glass from her and took his own sip. "I killed all of my mother's husbands. And every one of them, besides my father, was innocent."

She parted her lips.

"Each time my mother married, she would stay with the guy for a year or two, and then all of a sudden, her husband ended up raping or abusing her. At least that was what she would tell me. These were her bedtime stories, whispering the sick crap her ex-husbands would do to her. Something sickening always happened to dear mother, and I, the ever loyal, and protective son, I... " He drank some more of Dracula's Blood. Spicy cinnamon bit at his tongue.

He swallowed some more. "This isn't that bad."

"How did you figure out that she was lying?"

"Things stopped making sense. In her old age, she mixed up her lies. The guy who she'd said raped her, later had hit her. Things like that. Deceit and lies only last for so long before the light shines on them, and reveals the truth."

Diana gazed at him, never reaching for her glass or inching back in fear like she'd done before. "What happened, when you realized that she'd been lying?"

"I took her to the end of the property late at night, choked her... for a long time... and then I watched that devil burn up in flames." Water glazed over his eyes. It was his turn to finish the glass. "I take my time with my kills now. Usually. I spend months trying to make sure the person really *is* guilty. It's hard to do. More people get hurt, while I'm trying to decide if the person should die or not. Take, Maxwell. The nurse confessed his transgressions two months ago. That means that in that time, some more of his kids have been raped."

"But how do you ever know for sure?"

"I don't. That's one of the reasons why you're here. You're going to investigate, while I keep him busy."

"What do you expect me to do?"

"Snoop. It's what you do best."

Maybe, she was too drunk to feign ignorance. Instead, she grinned. "So you want your cat to stumble drunkenly along the foster home and sniff out clues?"

"And," He raised one finger. "I want you to see why I'm necessary."

"You want me to see if you're a necessary murderer."

"A hero."

"I don't name heroes." She targeted him with her gaze. "I only name serial killers."

"You still believe that's what I am?"

"Maybe."

"And what do you think of Maxwell?"

"I'm not sure."

Asher rolled his eyes. "Please tell me you can see through his silly sophisticated façade?"

Diana plucked another wine glass from a traveling waiter. "I don't know. He seemed pretty genuine to me."

Asher took the drink away, and offered it to another waiter. "Perhaps that's because now you'll be comparing every person to me. The atrocities you think I've committed. I promise you, my curious little cat, that you will understand one day. At least it's my sincere hope that you will."

Diana looked away from him.

"Stop."

She whipped her head in his direction. "What?"

"Stop thinking about it. Can you just let it go for tonight? Enjoy yourself? Isn't the truth what you live for? Doesn't it burn in your gut just as deeply as righting wrongs does for me?"

She pursed her lips together in defiance. She probably didn't want him to know that he'd pegged her so completely. It was easier for her to pretend he was a monster, when he didn't say things like that. It was so much harder to forget the lust coursing through her veins at the same time.

"For tonight, follow Cupid on his trail. Promise me that. No trying to run off and escape or whatever you'd planned on doing in the bathroom." He extended his hand. "Tonight, we work together."

"Together?" She grimaced at his hand. "I don't know how to use a bow and arrow."

"But you do know how to find the truth."

"I doubt you want that."

"Try me, Diana. See how far the rabbit hole goes when it comes to Asher Rice."

"Asher Rice?"

"My real name. Besides my mother, you're the only person that knows that fact. And now she's dead."

"Why did you tell me?"

"Because I put my faith in you. I—"

She put a finger to his lips. Her gaze softened and her face flushed. Whether it was from the alcohol or the honesty in his voice – he'd never know. She intertwined her fingers with his. "Okay, I'll help you out. Just for tonight."

CHAPTER SIX

DIANA

How do you escape a killer?
Be his friend.

Alcohol fogged Diana's thoughts, but she didn't care. The drinks were necessary, every last one. Her inhibitions needed to be lowered, in order to get through this night with Asher.

She wanted the alcohol to drown out the two parts of her body warring against each other. Fighting on whether or not Asher should be a part of her future.

Liquor always flooded the logical part of her brain. Logic wouldn't save her though, not when it came to Asher.

Dracula's blood ran through her veins. It made her strong, put some power into her step as she followed behind Asher and Maxwell.

How do you catch a pedophile?
Go to where the children are.

Like Asher commanded, she maintained a good distance between them, ducking into the ballroom's shadows or even hiding behind a group of chatting folks. By that time, everybody had more than enough of Dracula's Blood pulsing through them.

One woman had pulled her gown down a little and exposed a pink nipple to the fat, old man next to her. He'd snorted like a pig, fell into the big breast, and suckled on the tip like a hungry baby with its mother. A few around the craziness shrieked. Others gazed wickedly at the scene.

I should be walking in the other direction. I have a cellphone, money to get my ass off this island quick. I'm scared. That's why I'm following him. He's obsessed with me. I think so at least. Would he let me go, or would he follow me all over this earth, and have me in fear for years?

In that moment, Asher glanced over his shoulder, and she could've sworn, he spotted her. She'd been hiding by two tall men that were dressed like decrepit mummies. Gray bandages wrapped all over their body. Red eyes peered out of the top of each face.

Nodding, Asher turned around and went through a back door with Maxwell, talking about something and pointing in front of them.

The door shut behind them.

This is the moment. I can run the other way or move forward. Green or red pill, Diana? Which one?

She bit her bottom lip.

Red pill.

Diana was sure it was the cat inside of her, stretching and rising to attention.

She made her way through the crowd of endless designer

tuxedos and crimson gowns. That color red spread all over the ballroom—bloody silks, rubies sewed along hems, cherry hoop skirts, and scarlet pleats with sharp edges. If not for the elegance, the whole place could've served as the perfect backdrop to a party scene in a vampire movie.

Red pill for a red night. I'll wait a few seconds, before going outside and sneaking behind them.

She picked up another long stemmed champagne flute and stopped at a beautiful sculpture of two black bodies intertwined. She couldn't tell where one body began and ended—only that limbs, torsos, and heads blended together.

A female voice sounded on her right. "They call that sculpture, The Melding."

Diana looked beside her and saw a short Asian woman smiling.

"Oh? Is that what they call it?" Diana asked.

"Interesting isn't it? The two bodies seem to conjoin together."

Diana nodded in agreement. "Yes, it is. I've never seen something so... creepingly beautiful."

The woman laughed. "I suppose you could call it that."

"Well, have a good evening." Diana headed off toward the back door.

"Are you following Maxwell and Mr. Bishop?"

That question stopped Diana. She twisted around and faced the woman. "Excuse me?"

"I'm only asking because I'm supposed to follow you." She offered her hand. "I'm Maxwell's assistant, Theresa."

Diana shook it. "I like to keep Mr. Bishop in my sight."

"I wouldn't blame you." She whistled. "He's... simply gorgeous."

A little jealousy pinched at Diana's gut. She blamed it on the liquor.

Diana winked. "Maxwell wants *you* to keep an eye on *me*?"

"Yes." The woman looked proud to confess it. "You're a reporter. He hates them."

"Most business men hate reporters."

"Not the ones that don't have anything to hide."

And so your boss has something to hide, and you're just going to walk up and tell me this?

Diana calmed herself and sipped some of the champagne. Theresa had snared her attention, in the way that most informants did. Diana stood back and studied the woman. Instead of an immaculate gown, she wore a simple red dress with a big collar that revealed not one inch of her chest or cleavage. A big bow sat on top of her head and reminded Diana of Minnie Mouse. Black and white polka dots covered the flats on her feet.

"How long have you worked for Maxwell?"

"That's a complicated answer. We practically grew up together."

"Your families know each other?" Diana smirked. "Parents are college friends and all that jazz?"

"No." Embarrassment seemed to pinch at the corner of her eyes. "I don't know my family. Have you ever heard of the term *aged-out?*"

"No."

"It's what they call foster kids that never get adopted. They're the ones that stay in the system until they turn eighteen and have to survive on they're own."

"Because they're aged-out?"

"Yes. I was one of those kids."

"I'm sorry."

"No, don't feel bad for me." Theresa shook her head. The bow flopped with the movement. "Horrible things happen in the system. In some ways I was lucky to be transferred to Ovid Island's foster home, the one that Maxwell's family has run for over forty years. We celebrate the anniversary next month."

"That's amazing. I see what you mean now. Maxwell and you sort of grew up together."

"His father brought him around a lot and we all played together every summer. I don't want to bore you with my story. There was something that I wanted to ask you... away from Maxwell." Theresa looked around as if she worried someone else might see her talking to Diana. "I read your articles about Cupid."

Ice cold shock splashed across Diana's face. "You read about Cupid?"

"Yes. That's what the police and you have been calling him. It was announced this morning on the local news."

"Oh."

"Why didn't you write an article for the latest victim?"

"I-I've been pretty busy."

"Are you scared?"

"Scared?" Diana gritted her teeth. "You have no idea."

"I heard that Cupid left a message to you. The whole island has been talking about it. What did the message say?"

Diana scanned the people around them as if they were whispering about her right then. "The whole island knows about the message?"

"Yes."

Irritation turned her shock and fear all into a bundle of rage. "That should've been kept silent by the police."

"Too many people on this island are stuffing money into police officers' pockets. I knew by morning about most of the details. Everyone's afraid, even Maxwell, and I didn't think he could be afraid of anything. The cops are leaking details for money. Typical, right? The details of the message is the highest priced item on this island, tonight."

"Really?"

"Yes." Theresa came closer. "They're all afraid. You did that, Mrs. Carson."

"I didn't. Cupid did."

"But without you, we would've never known about him. The police would've taken forever to connect the killings. Everyone's afraid."

"Everyone shouldn't be. I believe Cupid has a particular type of victim... although I'm not a hundred percent sure. This killer is still a mystery to me."

For some reason, Theresa came closer and touched

Diana's arm. "I just want to thank you for your articles. No one else will speak up."

"No one else will speak up about Cupid?"

"No." Theresa shook her head. "No one else will state the obvious, that this Cupid is killing particular men. You listed them, and anyone who's been on this island for more than a few years, knows that those particular men... well... they weren't that good at all. Your article is scaring all of the bad men off the island. You and Cupid."

She held in her shock. "Me and Cupid?"

"I don't know if you know his identity. I hope you do because I worry about you."

Diana touched her chest. "Me?"

"Yes, the article could get attention from Cupid, if you don't know him. It's gotten attention from him. I mean goodness, he left you a message." Theresa looked at her. "What did the message say?"

"I don't want to talk about it."

"Of course. I understand." She patted Diana's shoulder.

"Thank you. Although the police aren't taking this seriously, I do think we should leave the details to the investigators and stay out of their way."

"Yes. I think you're right." She glanced at the closed door. "And you do have Mr. Bishop to keep you... protected. He's such a strong and big man."

Diana tossed her a fake smile. "Asher has really been supportive and kind throughout this whole process. He's helping me as I mourn my husband, one of Cupid's victims.

In fact, I should run off and catch up with them. I'd planned on scaring them a little. You know. We *are* partying at a Monster's Ball."

Theresa took her hand away from Diana and rolled her eyes. "Maxwell will surely love to be scared. He's a pro at jumping out of the shadows and scaring everyone. However, I'm the hide and seek champ, and have always been."

"Good for you."

"I try." She fussed with the bow on her head and stepped back. "Go ahead. There's no need to keep my eye on you. Maxwell is just on edge. He wanted me to follow you around, while Mr. Bishop and he were away. He's just being paranoid."

"Is he?"

"Since the last victim, he's beefed up security."

"Why would he do that?"

"I don't know." Her face changed into a neutral expression. "Why do you think he would do that, if Cupid is only killing bad men?"

With that last statement, Theresa smiled. "Have a good evening, Mrs. Carson. I can't wait to read your next article. You've gained a fan from me and many of the other Servs."

"Servs?"

"Servs is another term that you might not have heard of. It's what all the people who only work on this island call themselves. In the end, we're just nameless servants for these people. But, we keep our eyes open and our mouths shut." She sighed. "Some days, it's really hard to do that."

"Maybe, these... Servs should go to the police."

She chuckled. "You're a very funny person, Mrs. Carson."

And then Theresa left.

Did that really happen?

Diana had gained fame from her articles before. That wasn't what caught her off guard.

Theresa had a different angle. She believed that she knew who Cupid was, and it almost seemed to Diana that the woman hoped her boss would be the next victim.

Was that the liquor or my imagination? Or do I just want to believe this all, because maybe, just maybe it would make me feel okay for falling in... whatever I am with Asher?

With a renewed hope in the investigation, she hurried toward the backdoor, glancing behind her every now and then. If anything, she could convince Asher to not kill Maxwell tonight just by telling him the whole conversation.

He had brains. It would be stupid to go after Maxwell so soon after Theresa's assumption of Diana possibly knowing the identity of Cupid.

Theresa is probably watching me from some dark corner right now.

If Maxwell died tonight, Theresa would make some guesses and probably tell the police. Even if she was scared to talk, she'd have to confess that she saw her boss leave with Asher. It was just her job after all. And everyone knew that Diana had an interest in searching for Neil's killer. If Theresa told the police that Diana was monitoring both men's movements that would make the cops curious enough to turn their attention on Asher.

He couldn't kill Maxwell tonight.

Wait a minute. Isn't this what I should want? For Asher to get caught? What the hell am I thinking? I shouldn't try to protect him. I should do my best to make him slip up. Let my hands be clean of what I know.

She stopped at the door and gripped the knob.

No, no, no. If I do find out that Maxwell is guilty of hurting these kids, and Asher wants to kill him, I should let him. Theresa would be my witness. She'd help me prove that Asher was Cupid. I'd be free of his plans.

Relief didn't flow through Diana, just guilt twisting with pain.

Does Asher deserve it? Should Maxwell die? Wait a minute. Do I really want to protect a pedophile? Hell no.

She opened the door and rushed through, practically limping forward in the stilettos. Cold wind hit her face. All these plans filled her brain before coming outside, yet under the glow of the moon, something changed inside of her.

If Maxwell hurt those kids, then... I won't stand by to protect him.

She tiptoed forward. Masculine voices sounded up ahead. She followed that direction and hope no one else lingered in the bushes. Anytime a stick cracked or a leaf rustled, she jerked forward in fear.

Don't be scared, Diana. The monsters are in front of you.

It took several minutes to catch up with them. They'd

gone down a path decorated in sea shells. She'd given up, taken off her shoes, and crept the rest of the way.

When the voices sounded louder, she ducked behind a tree, waited a few seconds, and peeked.

Asher and Maxwell stood in front of a huge green house. At least she assumed it was them. Two dark figures were in front of the door—one tall and muscular, and the other small like Maxwell.

"I never take for granted where I came from." Maxwell's voice rose in the air. Keys jingled next. "This is why I want to make sure others never have to endure hardships. I want them to feel loved, encouraged, and supported."

Asher's dark voice came next. "You're a very kind man. Not many on this island are like you."

"Oh thank you, Bishop."

"Mr. Bishop," Asher corrected.

"Yes, Mr. Bishop."

"Thank you."

"Mr. Bishop, I disagree with you, however."

"You do?"

"There are many men on this island that love children as much as I do."

Let's hope not.

A sick shiver ran through Diana.

"That's exactly why I live on this island." Asher chuckled, and Maxwell joined along. "For all the many men on here and their love of children. I'm dedicated to children, myself."

"Right." Maxwell lowered his head. "Well, if you're ever interested in volunteering at the home, let me know."

"Tell me more about this volunteer program."

They both walked inside. The door remained ajar. No doubt, Asher made sure of that.

Holding her shoes, Diana tiptoed in the shadows, opening and closing the foster home door with a silent ease.

Maxwell and Asher were only a few feet ahead of her and around the corner. Their laughter drifted from the right and the floorboards creaked beneath her as she walked forward.

She froze but no one came toward her. No other sound filled the room. Just silence.

Where's the home manager, or whoever watches the kids in the evening?

Diana scanned the room. It was just a small space, used for nothing, it seemed, but entering and exiting.

This is a back entrance. Of course.

She checked the ceilings.

No cameras? I don't think so. Do you not want anyone seeing you coming and going through this entrance, Maxwell?

She headed over to the corner where the men's voices had come from and peeked. Nothing but empty hallway greeted her eyes. They'd probably entered a room or turned another corner.

She exhaled and went in the other direction. Adrenaline pumped through her veins. Sweat clung to the pits of her arms and stained the top of her gown.

This wasn't her first time sneaking into a building. And it certainly wasn't the first time adrenaline pumped through her as she did something she knew she shouldn't be doing. It was just her first time doing it all in a freaking gown. The pearls swished back and forth with the wispy garment. On a runway, it would have been great. During a snooping opportunity, not so much.

Where the hell do I start? Asher, you're insane. Go investigate, you say. Where? What? How? Hmmmm.

Black doors appeared on the right. Names hung on each one. Diana walked by all of them and then stopped at the one that read,

Maxwell Grayson

One fact reigned true for most rich people. They always kept their secrets right in their office, too lazy and comfortable in the fact that they had power and no one would stop them. Had they never read the novels where the bad guys always got it in the end?

"Please say it's open. Please say it's open." She turned the knob with ease. "No need to lock your office door, when you own the place? Stupid. Stupid."

She walked into pitch-black darkness and closed the door.

I wish I brought my pocket book with the tiny flashlight.

Then someone opened the door behind her. It all happened so fast. She jumped. A small person crashed into Diana. Right as she was going to ask who it was, they raised a huge object in the air and hit her in the head.

A sharp pain bit at the front of her skull, and all she could whisper before she collapsed to the floor was, "Cupid."

CHAPTER SEVEN

ASHER

Spending time with Maxwell had taken the last bit of patience out of Asher.

Finding no sight of Diana had pissed him off so bad, he clenched and unclenched his hands into fists within his pockets. He'd called her phone, texted several messages, checked every inch of the ballroom, and even stormed into all of the ladies' bathrooms, to a few women's horror. Granted, not all of the women minded.

There was no denying it. She was missing from Maxwell's party—not a single witness to account for where she was or where she could have gone. Even Maxwell's assistant, a short Asian woman, said she hadn't talked to or seen Diana at all the whole night.

He hadn't believed that she would actually do it.

Run away.

He'd been stern in his warnings, and her trembling lips persuaded his softer side. Plus, she had to know the consequences.

She's gone. What does this mean for me? Do I kill Maxwell now, so that I can focus all of my attention onto Diana?

Lust had blinded him, and her rosy scent had clogged his senses. He hadn't seen the deceit on those lips. No lies prickled from her fingers when they shook hands that night and agreed to work together on Maxwell. His heart bet everything on Diana, put it all out on the line, and handed over every ounce of his trust.

She loves me not.

Diana, his little bird had transformed back into a curious cat.

When had it begun?

Had she started shapeshifting in the limo, right as those sweet lips touched his? He hadn't seen it. Her soft black feathers remained, not thick cat fur. Sure, she'd been scared, but her feathers hadn't been ruffled. They'd lifted in the breeze.

When did it happen?

Had she shifted in the bathroom? Was it the song, that intense melody of possession and terror? Did those lyrics sink deep into her head like it did for him? That must've been when the claws pushed out of her bird feet. Feathers had sunk into flesh, molding into curiosity and sprouting black fur.

She'd come out of the bathroom as his cat, and he'd been too blind to notice.

Where are you Diana? Don't make me do this. Don't make me kill you. Please, I don't think I can survive. I barely did, after...

"Still haven't found her?" Maxwell held both of his hands together as if he'd just come out of praying. It made him look off. Something so spiritual as hands pressed together in prayer shouldn't exist on a vile man as him. It was an abomination, like walking into a church, stopping at a statue of the crucifixion, sticking a red lace bra around Jesus's neck, and writing on the lord's nailed-in palms, numbers of women that give the best blow jobs in town.

If Diana ran, I'll find her. It doesn't matter how much of a jump-start she has. Now, I'll kill Maxwell. It'll make me feel better.

"No, I haven't found her, yet." Asher took his hands out of his pockets. "Do you have any ideas?"

"N-no. Me?" Maxwell touched his chest. "Why would I have any ideas? I've told you everything I know."

Asher raised his eyebrows. The anger of Diana missing had pulled away the alcoholic haze he'd been walking in. Things started to make sense. Before they seemed to point in a more confusing direction.

Asher studied Maxwell some more. The man kept those hands in the prayer sign. Every few seconds, he checked the exit and then looked back at Asher.

Does he know something? Or do I just want to kill him so much that I'm hoping he has something to do with Diana's disappearance? Instead of wringing her beautiful neck, I can twist his the fuck off, and blame him for everything? Maybe, I'll do it regardless.

"Have you seen Diana?" Asher asked again, his tone deepening by the time he said her name.

"I've been with you most of the time."

"Very true." Asher nodded and then closed the distance between them.

Maxwell edged back and then bumped into the wall behind him. No one noticed what occurred between them. It was well past midnight. Only the drunks remained, dancing off beat to the music and stumbling around the dance floor like crazed fools. Everyone else had left.

"What are you doing?" Maxwell looked up at Asher, but didn't push him away, like any normal man would.

He's used to being dominated by men. Interesting.

"You're hiding something." Asher poked at Maxwell's chest the same way Diana had did earlier that night. "You don't want to fuck with me. Are you listening? You don't want to be my focus this evening."

"I-I have s-security all around me."

"You'll have blood all around you soon too." Asher put his mouth near the man's ear and whispered, "I could kill you right now."

"W-what?"

"I could slice your neck. It's dark. The music is loud. Even if your security came. You'd be dead. They'd catch me, sure, but you'd be dead. Blood everywhere. The police could come, but you'd be nothing but a lifeless corpse surrounded by a pool of your own filth. People would scream and alert someone to save you, but it would be too late. Do you know why?"

Maxwell's body quaked against him. "B-because I would be d-dead."

"Do you know anything about where Diana is at?"

Maxwell opened his mouth and then closed it.

"Walk with me." Asher snatched him up by the collar and pulled him toward the back.

"You're insane! What are you doing?"

Two men rushed to them. "Mr. Grayson, is everything okay?"

Asher dug his nails into the man's flesh on the back of his neck and whispered, "You tell them to leave. If not, I'll leave, but I'll come back, and you'll have no idea when, or how mad I will be."

"This is all insane." Maxwell struggled to get out of his hold. "There's no reason for this."

"Mr. Grayson?" one of the guards said.

Asher dug his nails in even harder and was sure he'd broken the skin.

"We're fine." Maxwell raised his hands in the air. "I think Mr. Bishop might have had too much to drink. I'm going to walk him to his car. Isn't that right, Mr. Bishop?"

"That's right." Asher nodded. "Let's just go out the back entrance. I don't want too many people seeing me this way."

Wrinkles spread across Maxwell's forehead. "Yes, we'll go out the back."

CHAPTER EIGHT

DIANA

Rope bound Diana to the leather chair behind Maxwell's office desk.

What the fuck?

She battled with the rope, but there were no weak spots. Her captor had skills.

Her hands were held securely to her sides. All she could do was press her fingers against her hips. She hadn't brought her phone with her, when Asher and she arrived at the Monster's Ball. She'd kept it in the limo. That very fact enraged her.

Always keep the phone near me. How many freaking times do I have to remind myself?

The door opened and stopped all of Diana's thoughts.

A petite silhouette stepped into the room. So small, it had to be a woman. The figure wore a dress and a... bow on her head.

Theresa.

It should've shocked her that Maxwell's assistant had

something to do with this, but nothing did anymore, not after finding out that Asher was Cupid.

A click sounded. The light turned on and bathed the little woman in a glow. "You said you were going to follow and scare them, not search around for information."

Diana glared at Theresa. "Did you do this?"

"What were you doing in Maxwell's office?" Theresa touched her bow as if it had fell from her head.

"Did you hit and tie me up?" Diana asked.

"Yes."

"Why?"

"No, Mrs. Carson, it's time to answer my questions." Theresa shut the door behind her. "What were you doing inside of Maxwell's office?"

"I was barely in here, before you rushed in and knocked me out."

"What were you going to do?"

"I had no idea it was even his office. I was just going to—

"Lies!" She yanked at the edge of her bow over and over. "His name is on the door."

Diana stared at Theresa's fingers. "I love that bow on your head. It reminds me of Minnie Mouse."

Theresa snapped her hands away from her head. "What were you hoping to find here?"

Think fast. Figure out what she wants, and get her to release me.

Diana considered their last conversation and cleared her throat. "I'm... hunting for clues."

"About Cupid?"

"Yes." Diana bobbed her head. "Of course. What else would I be searching for?"

The woman didn't move or respond.

"I believe Cupid is not a... what was that name you called people who worked on the island?"

Get her to talk with me. Get her to think that we are friends.

"They're called Servs," she said.

"Yes. The police think that Cupid is a Serv, some guy that works around the island and is fed up with all of these rich men. Do you think Cupid is a Serv?"

"I doubt it."

"Me too. I think it's a rich man."

"And that the rich man is Maxwell." She slipped her fingers against her bow again. "You think he is Cupid?"

"I... I think that Cupid could be Maxwell or any rich man on this island. I'm simply going around and investigating each one."

Theresa nodded. "And Mr. Bishop has been helping you."

It didn't sound like a question, so Diana chose not to answer. Instead, she decided to play along. "So... is Maxwell, Cupid? Is that why I'm tied up? Am I going to be his next victim?"

Theresa squinted her eyes at Diana. "What's fascinating is not that you're asking me something that is so ridiculous, it's that you don't even look scared. You're bound in a man's office, a person who you may think is Cupid, but you don't look nervous or afraid."

"I've been walking with fear all weak. It gets draining after a while."

Theresa pulled out her phone and typed.

Diana's heartbeat picked up. "Who are you talking to? Maxwell?"

"You and I might have made a grave mistake." The woman twisted her lips to the side and whistled. "I'm not really sure how we can get out of this without somebody getting hurt."

"What do you mean?"

Theresa tossed her a sad expression and placed the phone to her ear. "I just hope you're as smart as they say you are. Maybe, we can convince him that everything is okay. He doesn't like being lied to. He… he has a temper. And when he gets mad, it's bad. Very, very bad."

"Wait. Hang up the phone." Diana scooted forward in her chair, barely an inch, which made her bump her knee into the solid desk in front of her. "Who are you calling?"

"Maxwell."

"Hang up. Let's talk this through before we get the guys involved. Trust me. You don't want Asher involved. And we don't want to make Maxwell angry do we?"

Theresa hung up and stared at her. "Why not? The check he gave to the foundation has already been signed. I will apologize and Maxwell will forgive me as he always does. Now, you…"

"I'm not talking about a damn check. I'm talking about

our lives." Even though she talked, she wriggled her fingers, still searching for a weak spot in the binding. "And forget Maxwell, Asher is very protective of me."

"I've guessed as much. He's been storming around the ball room for hours."

"Hours? How long have I been knocked out?"

"Long enough. We figured he would've just thought you left, and went away, himself."

No. If he thinks I escaped, then he'll leave the island. It makes the most sense. He'd go to Miami, and have people check the airports or bus stops, maybe even cruise line ports. Car rental businesses would be next. He could hire hundreds of investigators to do the light work.

"Don't worry." She held out her hand as if to say stop. "I'm probably going to be the one punished, not you. I... just need you to lie a little."

"Yes. I can lie. I can do whatever you need me to." Diana gestured to the ropes. "I just need you to take these off."

"No, not yet. I have to get ahold of things first." She dialed the number again, and held the phone to her ear. "This isn't good. He's not answering."

"Maybe, Asher is with him. Does Maxwell know you have me in his office?"

"Yes." She frowned. "As soon as I followed you in here and realized you weren't going to do what you said, I got into the office quick and hit you with my purse."

"It's a very heavy purse."

She nodded. "I keep a gun in it."

"Oh." Diana tensed in terror. "Why did you hit me again?"

"I didn't know what you were doing." She returned her attention to the phone, tapping out something and sighing. "Maxwell relies on me to keep him safe. I have to keep my promise to him. It's my responsibility."

"Do you always just hit someone, when you want to know what they're doing?"

"Stop talking. I'm trying to focus." She slid her fingers on the phone's screen with one hand, with the other, she toyed with the end of her bow.

Get into her head, Diana. She's broken somehow. I mean for god sake, she's a grown woman dressed like Minnie Mouse. Something is wrong with her.

"I used to wear a bow like that, when I was a little girl." Diana gazed at the thing on her head as if it was a diamond ring. "Do you wear them a lot?"

"I try. Maxwell doesn't let me wear them much."

"Why not?"

She continued to mess with her phone. "He says it doesn't look professional."

Get her attention somehow.

"Do the kids like your bow?" Diana asked.

That snared Theresa's attention. "No. They don't."

"Why not?"

"Sometimes, kids are just funny that way." She returned to her phone.

"Right."

"Do you have kids?" she asked Diana.

"Yes, but not in the way you're talking about. My kids are my articles. I'm too selfish and irresponsible to be a mother." Diana gestured to the ropes. "I mean look at me. I always get in trouble. What exactly do you do for Maxwell again?"

Theresa eyed Diana with a haunting glare. "Why do you ask?"

"Why not? I'm just making conversation. Currently, my schedule has seemed to clear this evening. I'm all tied up with you." Diana wagged her eyebrows. "I'm all yours. I figured we could chat."

"Well, our chatting needs to focus on getting us both out of this situation without anyone being hurt—"

"Or dying?"

"I don't like to talk like that."

"Of course not." Diana smiled. "Me either, especially when the death could concern me. That's a real downer."

Theresa took her hand away from her head, put her phone back in her pocket, and sat down on the loveseat in front of her. "We'll have to wait until he calls back. I've done enough tonight. I should've just let you go into the office. All you wanted to know was that Maxwell wasn't Cupid. I just kept thinking you were going to hurt him in some way and so I... "

She offered Diana a sad look. "I'm so sorry. Let's try to figure out a good solution to this problem."

"A nice apology goes a long way. Personally, I feel like your apology was enough. All is well again. Untie me, and I'll go my way, and you can go your way. This was all just a big misunderstanding."

Theresa grinned. "Really?"

The word escaped her lips in pure desperation. "Yes."

The woman almost rose, lifting a little, and then she slumped back down. "I should wait until Maxwell lets me know it's all okay. He's already mad that I hit and tied you up."

"Well... don't you think that was a bit much?"

"I thought you might've been working with Cupid. Maybe, finding the victims for him. There's been talk around the island."

"Oh really? And what are the lovely people of Ovid Island saying these days?"

"Everyone knows Mr. Carson was horrible to you. People said that he dragged you all over this island—"

"That's metaphorically, of course, being that I would have whipped his behind, if he'd tried to put his hands on me."

Theresa giggled. "I believe you."

"Anyway, what is the island saying about Diana Carson?"

"That you might've figured out who Cupid was, contacted him, had the crazy person kill your husband, and then—"

"That's stupid."

"Yes, but scared people think up the dumbest things." She pulled out her phone and checked it.

"Anything?"

"Nothing. It's not like him to not answer for this long. When I text or call, he responds immediately."

Asher, did you kill him already?

And then, Diana decided to just blurt it out, "Maybe, Maxwell is having fun with the kids."

Quiet filled the space as if sound had raced away, scared to deal with the consequences of Diana's words.

"What do you mean by that?" Theresa asked.

"The island talks about other people too. They say Maxwell is very friendly with his kids. That he loves them more than an adult man should."

Theresa gasped.

"But then, like we've both already agreed, scared people say the dumbest things."

Saliva flew out of her mouth as she spat out the words. "Maxwell would never do anything bad to those kids."

"Good. I just wanted to make sure. Cupid is searching for his next victim. I have a big list of possible ones. Maxwell was on the list. I just had to make sure."

"Maxwell would never ever do anything bad to those kids. You have no idea, how many times he's saved me. Make sure you write about that." She jabbed her finger in Diana's direction. "Make sure you say in your next article about how much of a saint Maxwell is."

"I can't write while tied up, Theresa."

"You'll be released soon." She glanced at her phone and frowned. "As soon as he calls, I'll let you go. And then you write that article."

"I will."

Theresa stroked her hair and then as if unconscious of her

fingers' movements, tugged at the ends of her bow and played with it some more. Each time the woman's hand grasped at the bright red fabric, a thick tension sliced at Diana's gut.

Don't even think about it, Diana. She's going to free you. I'm sure Maxwell will say to just let me go, if they are really on the up and up. Don't look at that damn bow again.

She shut her eyes, and thought about all of the kids in the foster home. The very one that she sat in, bound to a chair. How fast had Theresa found the rope? Was it in the office or did she run off to get it? It couldn't have taken her that long.

Wouldn't it have taken a normal person a while to find something to tie a person up with? It's not like people just had a long piece of rope sitting around. Rope long enough to bind an average sized woman in her chair.

Unless…

Was this poor woman Maxwell's first victim? Had he stolen her innocence and youth in one fell swoop and made her crazy? Did he force her to watch as he did the same to the children of Ovid Island Foster Home?

Theresa hadn't even gagged Diana. Why not?

Diana let her gaze fall over the room. The walls looked thick. They probably held in the sound. They could've been specially made to make sure no one heard the things that went on, in an office that just happened to have a long piece of rope, hanging by.

Don't say anything else. Keep your mouth shut. Ride this out.

But she couldn't help herself.

"Where did you get the rope from?" Diana asked.

"Why?" Theresa leaned her head sideways and flicked the bow with her thumb.

"Just wondering. Really, I'm just making conversation."

"I got it out of my office."

"Cool. Your office is close to this one?"

"Right next door."

"Cool." Diana smiled. "You did a pretty good job of keeping me in this chair. It's pretty scary, in fact, how you were able to bind me so well, and in so little time."

"I've been tying knots since I was ten."

"For the Girl Scouts?"

"No."

Silence sat between them. A cruel expression spread across Theresa's face. "I think that you should stop asking me questions. It makes me nervous."

"I don't want to do that. When you're nervous, I think I will get nervous too."

"I agree."

I have to get out of this rope. I have to get out of this rope. Jesus Christ, and then I'm off this island. I don't care, what Asher says or does or... he can freaking come with me, if he likes. This island is evil. The whole place. What is wrong with her? She's been tying rope since she was ten! What does that mean? Did she mean it in an innocent way? No. I doubt it.

"Now, you're quiet." Theresa let her bow go, and stood up. "What are you thinking about?"

That was a loaded question. Her thoughts lingered between the possibility of getting chopped into little bits by this psycho and how weird it was that her fingers twirled around and around her bow.

"Your bow," Diana replied.

"That makes me nervous too."

"Why?"

Theresa paced back and forth in front of the couch. Every few feet, she checked her phone. "This isn't good. I should go see if he's okay."

"Who bought you your first bow?" Diana asked.

Was it Maxwell? Did he buy it for you to keep you quiet?

Theresa ceased with pacing and froze. "Why would you ask something like that?"

"I'm just into bows and making conversation. What's the big deal?"

Theresa marched over to Diana, kneeled in front of her, and placed her face a few inches from Diana's. "I don't want to talk about my bow either."

Diana should've jerked back or flinched, but she'd just seen a carved name in a dead body the night before. Even worse, she'd just fucked the man who'd taken the knife and sliced his name into the dying guy's chest.

Diana leaned her way and pressed her forehead to Theresa's. Their skin smoothed together, and only Theresa shivered.

Their eyes were right in front of each other.

Now, it's time to bluff. You've done this before. She's

weak, in some ways. Tear her up. Get inside her head.

Diana whispered, "Do you see fear in my eyes?"

"No." Theresa never moved her face away. "You make me nervous."

"I don't know Cupid, but I have other friends. If they think I'm gone, then that means, they're hunting."

"Hunting?"

"I bet they have Maxwell."

"No!" She fell back and dropped to the floor, rubbing her bow over and over. "Who is it?!"

"Untie me."

"Where is he?"

"Unfucking-tie me now!"

Theresa punched her in the face, so hard, Diana and the chair crashed to the ground. Carpet scraped against her skin, blood coated her tongue.

Diana spit it out and screamed. "Help! Help!"

Theresa walked over to where she'd fell, and kicked her in the stomach. Pain exploded through Diana's body. "Who has him?"

"Help!"

"No one can hear you, stupid woman. What did they do to him?"

"The same thing they'll do to you." Diana laughed like a mad woman. "They have a tracker in me. And you'll never know where it is!"

More bluffs, keep them coming. Make her believe.

"I can feel the tracker working. It's vibrating around my

back." Diana chuckled and sang, "You're going to die! You're going to die!"

"Stop it! Stop it!"

"Untie me!"

Theresa dropped her hands and then whispered, "Okay."

Diana tensed, too scared to utter another sound.

"They better not have touched Maxwell. Is that why he's not answering? He always answers." She hurried over to her pocket book and pulled out a small gun.

Oh yeah. I forgot about that.

She pointed the gun at Diana. "You better not do anything, or I'll shoot you, and leave you somewhere to die."

"I guess we're not friends anymore, huh? No exchanging of bows or anything like that this Christmas."

Theresa kicked Diana in the gut again.

Diana cried out in pain. Raw heat scratched at her throat.

Yet, Theresa did as she'd promised. She untied the rope as Diana lay sideways on the ground, trying to remember how her stomach felt before it had been kicked in several times.

Theresa kept the gun in one hand, and unloosened the rope with the other. How at ease she looked, just a twist here and a turn there. The knots loosened seamlessly like she'd just completed a Rubik's cube.

"There you go." Theresa yanked the rope away from Diana's arms, but still hadn't freed her legs.

It didn't matter.

As soon as Diana had a free hand, she launched for Theresa and screamed. Diana grabbed ahold of that ugly bow and refused to let go as she slammed the woman's head down on the desk, the chair still attached to the bottom half of her body.

They both fell. Diana crashed to the ground. Theresa dropped on the table. The gun tumbled onto the carpet.

Diana rushed to get the gun.

"No!" Theresa kicked it away and jumped on her. "Give me back my bow!"

"Fuck you!" Diana bit the side of her face and sank her teeth into that jaw until she could taste blood and anything else on her tongue. She refused to let go.

Fuck you! Fuck you!

She would not let this crazy bitch win. She would not be destroyed by this woman. Not after all she'd gone through.

Theresa beat at Diana's face, but Diana wouldn't let go. Like an aggressive dog, she locked her jaw onto the woman's cheek and relished in Theresa's wails.

Blood filled her mouth. The nasty warm liquid spilled over her lip, and Diana could no longer take it. She let go. Theresa fell back, grasping at her face like it was on fire and screamed over and over.

Something still lay between Diana's teeth. She spit the meat out and vomit rumbled in her stomach.

I bit off some of her cheek! Jesus! I have to get out of here before I throw up all over myself.

Still holding the bow, she raced for the door. Her fingers fumbled with the doorknob, but as she unlocked it, Theresa slammed into her. "Give me back my bow!"

"Take it." Diana beat at the wound on Theresa's face, hoping it burned worse than the kicks that she'd received. "Take your bow, bitch! Take it!"

She flung the bow at Maxwell's desk. And the craziest thing happened, Theresa twisted around and dove for the bow like a dog jumps after a flying Frisbee.

And then,
Diana ran.

CHAPTER NINE

ASHER

Asher held his limo door open for Maxwell. "Sit in the vehicle with me, for a few seconds."

Maxwell rubbed the back of his neck. "I will not."

"You will."

"Mr. Bishop, you've taken this situation far enough. I allowed you to drag me outside, due to your drunken stupor and kindness to my foundation, but I will not be a party to this anymore. Good evening." Maxwell tipped his head and turned

Asher looked around.

Valets brought cars back and forth to the entrance far away.

Maxwell knew he'd be safe out here. Too many people could witness something going wrong. The man believed he'd be fine with Asher inside of the ball and outside. A murderer prowled the island. Everyone had their senses perked and ready to catch anything odd or strange.

Going unaware would be harder now.

"Have a safe ride home, Mr. Bishop." Maxwell stalked off.

"I will, but I wonder if you will." He got in the car and shut the door.

Maxwell shook his head and headed back to the ball.

Asher wasted no time and tapped the divider that separated him from the driver. "I need you to drive off and park somewhere close by."

"Okay, sir."

"Keep your phone near you, and be ready to speed back to me, when I call."

Asher's driver nodded and obeyed as he always did. "Okay."

His name was Flame, and he'd been working for his mother and him for years. He'd been the first driver after the death of her first rich husband. Gray outlined his temples where black strands used to be.

Worry etched along his blue eyes. "Will you need anything else sir?"

"No, but thank you."

Asher never called the man Flame, never referred to him with a name at all. For some reason, he didn't think Flame liked that title, or the past that came with it. And the man had to have seen a lot in his life, because for all the years that he'd worked with Asher, never had he opened his mouth or looked scared.

And he'd seen plenty with Asher too—blood covering Asher's hands and tears spilling from his eyes after he killed his mother. That night, Asher had limped back to the limo, for no reason at all. He could've simply returned to his mansion.

Yet, he chose the limo, and asked Flame to drive.

And the old man got out of the limo, nodded his head, and opened the door, but before Asher ducked inside, the man wrapped his arms around Asher and hugged him for a long time, under the moonlight.

No words ever passed between them.

A minute later, Flame let go, Asher got in the car, and they drove for hours.

"I'll wait for your call." Flame's voice brought Asher back to the present moment.

Just in case, Diana had actually escaped, he decided to ask Flame a question. "Did you happen to see my date leave?"

"No, sir."

"Okay." Asher slipped out of the other side of the limo, where no one standing in front of the Ovid Island Art Museum would see him. He stayed low to the ground and crept to the bushes on the other side of the driveway. Once he got behind them, his limo drove away.

Maxwell probably watched my limo speed off. If something is up, then Maxwell will head off, somewhere. If I'm wrong, then Diana really left me...

and I hope she knows how to run, really fast.

He swallowed down the bile that rose in his throat and made sure to get a good view of the museum's front and back doors. Luckily, the limo parking was located on the side of the building, and provided an excellent view.

Before Asher could sit on the ground, something glimmered from the woods that were between Maxwell's foster home and the museum. He squinted his eyes. Light bounced off of a red gown, as a woman stumbled forward, fell into the ground, jumped up, and ran some more.

Without thinking, Asher rose from the bushes and screamed, "Diana!"

Out of the blackness, Diana ran toward him. That beautiful red dress torn at the bottom, caked in dirt and debris. Pearls fell behind her as she ran toward him.

"Asher!"

He rushed her way.

Even from two yards away, Asher recognized the terror in the step, that odd stumble through fear. His heart pounded and his veins grew thick with fury. Someone had hurt her. Someone besides Maxwell.

Blood dripped from her nose.

He crashed into her like a linebacker would, smashing into her small body, grasping at those hips, and dragging them both down to the ground.

"Ah!" She pushed him away, trying to get up.

"What happened to your nose?" He grabbed her face with both hands and examined her brown skin for more injury. Her eye looked swollen, and her lip was split. "Who? Just tell me who?"

"We have to get out of here!"

A shot rang in the air, far off in the woods.

A woman shrieked in front of the museum. "Did you hear that, Norman? It sounds like a gun."

"Shit." Asher released Diana, jumped up, and helped Diana rise. "Too many witnesses."

"No, that's good." She straightened her tattered gown and held his hand. "She won't shoot us out here."

"She?" he growled.

Footsteps stomped all over the place. Cars honked. A few people screamed. Most of the noise came from the front of the museum. Police sirens blared far away, but Asher didn't have to be a genius to know that they were coming to the Monster's Ball.

Everyone's on edge. The police have something to prove. I can't make any more mistakes.

"Let's go." He guided her toward the parking lot and pulled out his phone to call his driver.

"Mr. Bishop!" Maxwell's voice came from behind them.

Asher turned.

Maxwell's same bodyguards flanked him.

"I see you've found, Mrs. Carson." Maxwell did his best to hold in that frown, but Asher could tell that it had almost faltered. "Good. I'm glad you're safe."

"I *am* safe." Diana tucked her hair behind her ear. "I had a tumble in those woods over there. It's very dangerous."

She's saying nothing about who hurt her. Is this a performance for the security or Maxwell? What's going on?

"You should be careful over there." She pointed to the woods.

A few people hurried their way. Chatter fled from everyone's lips.

"Marjorie says there were gunshots." A fat man held his hand to his chest as if he'd been hyperventilating.

"Don't worry." Maxwell waved the man's comment away and turned to Asher. "The police have been called. Everything is fine. I'm sure it's all okay."

You're a very cocky man, Maxwell. I like to make cocky men bleed. And the best sounds come from their mouth when they bleed. It's a symphony.

Maxwell's confident expression faltered.

Can you hear my thoughts? Or do you see your death in my eyes? The smart ones always see it, days before it comes. What do you see?

Both men just stared at the other, as a crowd gathered around to discuss the possibility of a gunshot. Valet worked over time in that moment. The hysteria ended the Monster's Ball, and had everyone on edge.

"Well, I didn't hear a gun shot at all." Diana's words cut through the air and stopped Asher and Maxwell's face-off.

"You didn't?" a woman asked on her right. "Marjorie said it came from behind the museum."

"Where's Marjorie?" Diana asked.

"She just left," another replied.

"No doubt full of Dracula's Blood," Diana joked. "After a few of those, I bet anyone could hear a gun shot, or even more. I, myself, got lost around the museum and tore my dress."

She pointed to the ripped hem. "I think I would've heard something as I fell drunkenly to the ground."

People laughed. No one wanted a person with a gun in the woods. It was always easier for people to believe the best, than the scenario of them being in danger.

"Either way, I'm exhausted." She held Asher's hand. "Please, take me home, Mr. Bishop?"

Others went off into more conversation about Marjorie probably hearing nothing at all.

"You know Marjorie pulled her gown down earlier this evening," a man offered. "She had it all out, and showing it to the world."

"Who knows how much she'd been drinking by then." A woman fanned herself. "And she's managed to get us all upset, and then she just rushes away. That's *so* Marjorie."

Asher and Diana slipped away. She tightened her grip on him and continued to limp forward.

"Let me carry you." Asher stopped them.

"No."

"It goes with the story of you tripping and falling."

"I don't care. I don't want you to carry me."

"Why not?"

Her hands shook. "I just need to walk on my own right now."

"Who hit you?"

"Theresa."

"Who the hell is that?" he asked through clenched teeth.

"Maxwell's assistant."

"Mr. Bishop!" The man himself, Maxwell, rushed over to them. "Are you leaving so soon?"

Diana let go of Asher's hand and glared at the man. "Be fucking careful, Maxwell. Very, very careful."

Maxwell raised his hand.

The two security guards that had been following him, stopped, turned around, and walked back to the gathering crowd.

Asher quirked his eyebrows.

Diana pointed a finger at him. "Did you know that she had me in your office?"

Maxwell checked Asher's face.

"I would answer her questions," Asher said. "If you think I'm scary, well, then you've never pissed off the right woman."

"Did. You. Know?" Rage blazed out of Diana's gaze.

Asher swallowed and was relieved to see his limo pulling in. Diana looked ready to kill, and with the blood that had been dripping down her nose, he'd let her do whatever she needed.

Maxwell exhaled. "I knew that she had you in my office, but I didn't understand—"

"What? That she'd tied me up?" Diana stepped toward him. "That she kicked and beat me?"

Maxwell crossed his arms over his chest. "The police are coming. Maybe, you should press charges against her. Or do you have secrets that you don't want anyone to find out about?"

Her next word was a hiss. "Meaning?"

"There's talk that you know who Cupid is. That maybe you know who he is going to kill next. I don't know. People gossip."

She widened her mouth into a murderous grin. "People do gossip, but Maxwell, sweetheart, I've heard things too. And maybe, just maybe, you should consider getting your will in order."

Asher's cock hardened in his pants, never had he seen her so wild and pissed off.

Maxwell cringed. "I don't like to be threatened, Mrs. Carson."

"Then you should have thought about that before sending Theresa after me."

"I didn't," he said. "She acted on her own accord, as she always does."

Three police cars drove up to the front of the art museum.

"You may not want the police to go near your foster home tonight." Diana smirked. "Have a good night, Maxwell."

She limped off and Asher followed like a well-trained puppy.

CHAPTER TEN

DIANA

The ugliness of Ovid Island shined strong in Diana's eyes that evening.

As the limo traveled, Diana knew, without a doubt that there were monsters walking among the rich and elite on the Island.

These men,
they were less than cockroaches,
and they deserved to pay for their sins.

Asher hadn't said anything since they drove off.

She also remained silent, too much had happened for her to make sense of it all. Theresa filled her mind most of the drive. Someone hurt Theresa during her time at Maxwell's family foster home. The crazy woman couldn't stop touching that bow, and she had serious rope skills. The sicko bound Diana up too fast. Maxwell's office had soundproof walls. Theresa's loyalty to Maxwell seemed based on a sickness.

What type of assistant beats a person on the head and then ties them to their boss's chair, for him to come and deal with it? Those two have done bad things. Someone has to stop them, but I have no proof, besides her attacking. And I would need proof to get at a man as wealthy as Maxwell.

Unless...

Fucked up things traveled in her head. So many made-up scenarios of what those two could have done to so many powerless kids in their homes. How many times had they used that rope on a child? How many hours did someone scream in that soundproof office?

And what can I do, when I have no proof of this? That nurse who told Asher about the syphilis cases is probably long gone. If she didn't talk then, why would she talk now? And all I have is my gut feeling. These cops on this island don't even want to investigate when they have actual evidence. They would just sit there and laugh at my "gut feeling."

Asher's dark voice broke the silence. "Are you going to tell me what happened?"

Diana pulled her view from the window and faced him. "I want you to kill him. You were right."

"What?"

She grabbed onto his arm with such intensity, she thought her fingers might burn right through his suit jacket, through the thick muscle beyond his skin, maybe to his very bone. "I want you to kill Maxwell. I want you to make him suffer like those poor children have."

Asher blinked before answering. "Okay."

"Just okay? No explanation for why or... I don't know... a plan?"

"I already judged Maxwell." He grabbed her chin and lifted it so that her gaze met his. "You were the one that needed to be convinced."

She parted her lips, but he spoke before she could say anything else.

"His assistant hurt you?" Still holding her chin, his gaze examined her face like a concerned doctor.

"Yes, but I hurt her too. I bit out some of her cheek. Anytime she smiles, she'll think of me."

"Good. Don Quixote would be proud."

"You're never going to let that Don Quixote thing go, are you?"

"Not until I understand what the hell it means."

"There is no understanding it."

"Clearly." He moved in closer and caressed her mouth with his. "I thought you left me. I thought you ran. I thought I would have to..."

A shiver ran through her. "What?"

He sucked on her bottom lip. "I'll kill the assistant for you."

"No." She shook her head. "Don't do that. She's just as damaged as the kids are. Something isn't right in her head. If Maxwell is gone, then she may be able to thrive in a healthy way. Who knows how much abuse she's dealt with in her life?"

"Let me know if you change your mind. I would kill anybody for you."

"Asher, don't say things like that." She attempted to pull her face away from his grip, but he wouldn't let her go.

"You can't deal with the guilt of a murder on your hands?"

"I don't want you killing for me."

"Just Maxwell?"

She turned her attention to his hands, unable to look at him in the face. "Just Maxwell."

He frowned. "Do you want a message from Cupid? Hearts? Diamonds in the skin? Maybe some—"

"Why are you saying this?"

"I'm not insane. You're acting like I have no control. Sure, you want me to take this man's life, because now you've finally agreed with me that the police won't do anything, yet something needs to be done. Cupid needs to draw back his bow. Is that true?"

Her voice was a soft whisper. "Yes."

"But you don't want to get your hands dirty either?"

"What is that supposed to mean? Do you want me to clean off your bow and arrow, after you're done? Should I make you a special killed-a-pedophile cake?"

"No. I just want you to be able to look me in the eyes and stop flinching in fear or shaking every time I come close to you."

"You scare me. I can't help it."

"I don't care about what other people think, but when it

comes to you," he nipped at her bottom lip, "I fucking care to the point where a pain grows in my chest and I can't stop it from exploding and taking me down with it."

"What do you want from me?"

"To stop being scared."

"I can try."

"That's all I need, Diana. That's all I need." He devoured her mouth, and everything else disappeared.

The limo cruised along Ovid Island, rocking them as they tasted each other's lips and touched the things that they'd both been craving to feel again. Fingers tore back fabric and revealed hungry flesh that ached for a wicked tongue and tiny bite. Her dress sat on the floor in several huge pieces of ruby pearls and ripped silk.

Neither were patient. Diana yanked away Asher's jacket and tuxedo shirt as if they were nothing but thin pieces of paper. He was forced to help her with taking his clothes off, just so he wouldn't get injured in the process.

Moonlight glistened over the taut lines of his muscles on his arms and chest. Her pussy clenched at the sight, moistened so bad that when he dipped his finger between her opened legs, she damn near roared.

"You're so creamy." He lathered her arousal with his fingers and tasted the wetness, groaning as he sucked on his index finger. "I'm going to lick you until you scream my name."

He didn't wait for a reply. Instead, he dove between her thighs and pulled her leg up. She scooted forward and laid down, her back smoothing against the limo's leather seat.

"Put your legs in the air and then touch your toes."

She smirked. "What is my motivation?"

"I just want to do this to you." He stuck his long tongue out and lapped at an imaginary something in front of his face.

She took her time, lifting her legs and then spreading them wide so that she could touch her toes with her fingers. It left her so exposed, completely bare for his eyes to see it all, everything that rested between those thighs.

He ran his fingers through his curls, pulled out his phone, and pressed some number.

She let go of her toes.

"No." He grunted. "Don't move."

"Well, you're about to make a phone call."

"No. I'm about to make sure that I'm not interrupted." He held the phone to his ear and talked to the person on the other line. "Yes, I know we're close to the house. Just drive past it and keep driving until I tell you to stop."

He hung up and slung the phone onto the floor. "Now for my flower."

"I'm your flower?" She held onto her toes and got comfortable in that position—her on her back, her legs spread wide and in the air.

"This is my flower." He traced her moist fold with his fingers. "These are the petals." He spread them and toyed with her clit.

"Oh," she moaned.

"This is the diamond that the petals protect." He circled

her clit some more and she rocked into his hands, biting her lips.

"This is the beautiful stem." He guided his fingers down to her center and entered, in and out, in and out, wetness sloshed against his rhythm and disrupted the sound of her rapid heartbeat and his steady breathing.

Moaning, she let go of her toes and tried to get up, get more of whatever he was doing to her. But, he kept her down, dove toward her center, and buried his lips into her flower, sucking on the petals like they held an elixir for immortality.

Oh God. How did I ever breathe without this man?

His mouth found the diamond next. He drew the hungry bundle of sensitive nerves into his mouth, and with his tongue, he delivered ripples of pleasure.

So many noises fled her lips. "Asher. Oh baby. Yes, right there. Lick it."

Deep groans sounded from his throat as he feasted on her pussy as if her enjoyment turned him on even more.

His tongue was a tornado, her pussy the small deserted town that got swept up in its destruction—wind whipping, pleasure slipping, and chaos wet and moist.

Jesus! We're not in Kansas anymore, Toto.

Her laughter mingled with her moans. She was delirious. Real shit had occurred earlier, things that would make the average person's blood boil and explode. Now she lay in the back of a limo with a sexual god carved in muscle.

Asher paused and rose above Diana, his lips dripping with her. "You think my tongue is funny?"

"God, no."

"Then why did I hear a giggle?"

"I was thinking of the Wizard of Oz and your talents with... everything, all... oh just never mind."

"You're thinking of the Wizard of Oz as I pleasure you with my tongue?"

"Just ignore that."

"At least it isn't Don Quixote."

"Asher." She grabbed his face and pulled him down to her, his warm body smoothing against hers. "Fuck me."

"Okay, Dorothy."

Laughing, she hit his back. "No, you're Toto."

Growling, he grabbed ahold of his hard cock and pressed into her secret lips. "Who am I?"

Her body hummed in anticipation. "Just fuck me."

"Who am I?" He pressed his cock to her opening. It was so hot, the tip warming her up and making her wriggle within insanity. "Who am I, Diana?"

A soft whisper pushed out of her. "Asher."

"No, that's not my name."

"Asher, please." She could barely deal with him stalling anymore. She needed something—his lips, teasing fingers, talented tongue, or that hard, yummy cock that seemed to spread her all the way open and reveal more to him than any other man she'd ever been with.

He stared down her shaking body and grinned. "Interesting."

"Please."

"I won't push it tonight, but you will say my name."

"Yes. Yes. Now give it to me," she begged.

And he did,

all night.

The limo drove for hours, rocking and drumming an erotic beat that no one on the streets could ignore, as it sped by. Thankfully, not many people wanted to walk the dark streets anymore.

Yet, the limo traveled along Ovid Island, moving in a large circle around the land, passing things again and again, until night changed to day, sun bled into the darkness, and Diana's voice was stripped from her lips.

She'd screamed
and begged,
moaned and cried,
all night.

Asher never released her from the passion of their bodies slipping and sliding against each other.

He never let her go, never let her catch her breath

or take a nap

or have a few feet of space between them

or even to look down for a few seconds and make sure that her pussy was still there.

He conquered and destroyed the last bit of will she'd had left.

He never let her go.

First, they made love until she sang out her orgasm.

Then he turned Diana around, put her on all fours, and pounded into her, her ass deliciously bumping against his balls, her breasts bouncing in his hands as he grabbed them from behind and whispered over and over in her ears,

"I own you."

And the minute he said it, Diana knew it was true.

He owned her.

CHAPTER ELEVEN

CUPID

In Asher's bed, Diana slept on his chest.

With the white silk sheets rippling around her, she served as a beautiful piece of art—chocolate skin floating in vanilla, just begging to be tasted.

Asher ran his fingers through her long, black waves. It trailed around her face and some of the soft strands fell on his arm.

A few times, she shuddered in his arms and whispered about blood. In those moments, he'd hold her body close and kiss her forehead. Usually a sigh escaped her lips, and then she'd drift back into her calm dream world where hopefully lavender castles flew on sparkling clouds.

I hope you're having sweet dreams.

He could feel the heat of her skin,

the beating of her heart,

the ragged breaths that moved in and out of those lush lips.

Her scent permeated the air and made him think of spring. There were times, in his childhood, when spring came, and Mother left him alone to run outside among the flowers. He would grab sticks to trace his name between the cracks of battered pavement, fall down in the tall grass lot across the street from his old apartment building, lay on his back, spread his arms and legs wide, close his eyes, and just listen to the buzz of the bees and whistling breeze through the trees.

That morning triggered the same sensation. Peace flowed around him. Clouds hovered in the room as if no ceiling or walls existed. Instead of a bed, Diana and him lay within a field of daisies, so white and bright, he could barely see.

Diana had given him permission to kill.

And in that moment, something snapped inside of him. Prior to her permission, a wall stood between them, dark brick cemented by foreboding. When she asked him to take Maxwell's life, the wall crumbled, brick by brick, falling down to the ground. Dust lay at his feet, and in his heart, that uncoiling darkness dissipated into nothing, just faded smoke on a windy day.

She accepted him.

She encouraged him.

She was his.

He owned her, and he meant every damn word.

I've waited long enough. I should get up.

But the soft rhythmic breaths of Diana's slumber spilled over him like a blanket. For the first time in his life, the hunger for blood didn't overcome him. It tapped a little at his rib cage, but nothing more. Still, he climbed out of bed to grab his bow and arrow from the closet.

Death could not wait.

He had all the confirmation he needed, thanks to Diana.

Besides, he wanted to honor her wishes.

The white, silk sheets slipped away from his nude body as he rose. His erections loved the smooth fabric and probably thought that it might be a better idea to get back in bed, and maybe, wake up Diana.

No. Let's take care of this, and then I'll take care of her again. She'll need her rest for what I want to do to her. Last night was just the beginning.

Lust crashed into him, and he was no longer sure if it was his usual craving for blood or this new sensation beating inside of him.

Focus on what you need to do to Maxwell. Get Diana out of your mind right now.

And just like that, the dark hunger returned, no longer a faint echo. It poured into him, thickening with each second as he stepped into the closet.

In the far back of the space lay his bow and arrow, which sat upon a locker full of other fun things—wigs, fake tattoos, a compartment of make-up, and various folded costumes. Today he would be a regular Ovid Island Cable guy.

He opened the bottom drawer with his key and pulled out a worn jacket with the emblem sewed on the back—three blue circles around an island set in white. The company name was under the logo. He took out the matching white and blue hat.

What hair color should I be today? Hmmm. Shall I go au natural or exotic?

He yanked at the other drawer stacked with tons of concealers and body paint.

There'd been times when he'd tanned his skinned and donned short afros as he ducked in and out of apartments at night.

No. I better not. Too many rich men have died. If they think a black man is doing it, they'll disrupt every poor community in Miami and Fort Lauderdale over these murders.

He closed the drawer, but not before taking out green eye contacts, a black beard, and a shaggy black wig. Killing during the daylight always made him a bit nervous. He hoped the extra precautions would save the rush job.

Tip toeing around, he dressed and transformed into Dale Sampson, a trusted man that took cable installation seriously. Green glimmered over Asher's blue eyes. Shaggy black strands outlined his face and fell to his shoulder.

And just to be safe and get in character, Asher created the cable guy's bio in his mind.

Dale relished in heavy metal rock, after all, and although middle aged, he could not grow out of the phase. With a marker, Asher wrote AC/DC on his fingers, each letter huge and near his fingertips. If anybody came close, they'd remember those odd tattoos more than his face. It was little things like that, which always tied up the police.

Asher stuffed the same old pack of cigarettes in his back pocket like he always did. People were so damn judgmental. They wouldn't think twice about calling in a tip about a grungy forty-something with a pack of cigarettes in his hand. But if Asher Bishop walked out of the same place, more than likely there'd be no consequence.

Still, he didn't want to take the chance that he could be wrong.

If someone spotted him, they'd think he was a man with a drug habit, maybe a high school drop out that somehow stumbled into the job. To a millionaire, working for a cable company was just as menial as cleaning toilets.

They'd assume Dale was a lazy smuck, and dismiss him without taking another look.

Finished with his creation of Dale, Asher put on a book bag full of extra clothes, grabbed his bow and arrow, and then left through the back entrance where his motorcycle remained. Almost no one knew Asher had a bike, or that he could ride it.

Asher rather liked that he was full of secrets. No one could ever claim he was boring.

He took out his phone and typed.

Asher: *Where is he?*
Flame: *Foster home. There was a benefit breakfast.*
Asher: *People still there?*
Flame: *No. Not even the kids.*

Asher: *How sure are you that he's alone?*

Minutes passed, before his driver replied.

Flame: *80%*

Asher said no more, not wanting to get his driver in trouble, if something happened and they confiscated his messages. He'd involved the driver in enough of his nightly activities. If anyone could pinpoint him as Cupid, it would be Flame. The man had seen enough and taken him to several places to do his work.

When they'd returned home last night, Asher asked more of him than he should. He told Flame to find Maxwell and follow him until Asher called.

Asher jumped on his motorcycle, but before starting it up, he pulled out his phone and typed in a text.

Asher: *Take the rest of the week off.*

Flame: *Are you sure?*

Asher: *Yes.*

Right as Asher put his phone back in his pocket, it rang.

"Hello?" Asher said.

"Have I done something wrong, sir?" Flame asked.

"No, not at all. I just think I've pushed you far enough. You've been busy all week. Have you gotten any sleep?"

"Definitely."

"Then take a break."

"But..."

Asher raised his eyebrows. This was the most conversation he'd ever had with the man. Usually, they talked for no more than a few seconds.

"But, what?" Asher asked.

"Do you think you can trust her?"

"Her?"

"Mrs. Carson."

"Do you think that I shouldn't?"

"I'm not sure, sir. I just... don't want you to get in trouble."

"No?"

"No, sir. If you get in trouble, then..."

"You would. No, I can make sure that my activities will never fall on you. I have plans in place that involve us both, if things ever got hot on this island or anywhere else."

"Sorry. It's just that when I started with you years ago, I'd just got off of probation and I can't go—"

"Nothing will come to you. Trust me. Do you?"

"Yes, sir. It's her that I'm worried about."

"I understand. Do you have a reason for this distrust?" Asher asked.

"No, sir. It's just that some people aren't built for certain things, and some are."

"I would never involve her."

"Oh, I'm sorry, sir. I thought that you and she... you know, were going to be together."

"We are," Asher declared.

Silence sat on the line for a few seconds.

"Then I hope that she is built for these certain things."

"Me too."

"And I would feel comfortable with not taking a week off right now. If that is okay with you. I would like to stay close to you."

"That's fine, but get some rest."

"I will, sir."

He hung up the line abruptly. He'd already shown too much sentimentality toward Diana. He couldn't let himself get wrapped up in another personal matter. He just couldn't. There was too much to attend to.

Asher sat on the motorcycle and stared up at the sunlight hitting his bedroom window. Diana still slept in his bed, comforted by the exhaustion of their sex last night.

Would she be okay with me killing him right now? It must be yes. She told me to do it. Should I wait? No. She doesn't want to know too much. But is that wrong? Should she want to know? Is she really built for my life?

Asher took out his phone, yet again and typed his driver.

Asher: *After your rest, stay close to Mrs. Carson.*
Flame: *Follow her?*

Unease sat at the bottom of his stomach.

Asher: *Make sure she doesn't leave the property, unless it's with you, and let me know when and where she goes.*
Flame: *Yes, sir.*

It barely took him thirty minutes to get everything in

order.

There we go. I'm ready.

God yes, the hunger had returned for sure. Diana was only a memory within the fog of the need to kill. Like all the other moments right before he drew his bow, Asher craved that coppery scent of blood, yearned for it to spill, to pool around Maxwell's corpse.

It mattered that it was Maxwell and no one else. He was done with taking the breath away from innocent people.

And because the man represented so much evil—a demon that gnawed on children—Asher would take his time with him and leave his mark on the pedophile, inch by disgusting inch. Maybe, he'd let Maxwell beg for a while and hope for life, just to yank it from his sick, grasping hands. No matter the how or when, Asher would make Maxwell pay for the lives he'd ruined.

He'd save those foster kids. Only God knew how much those kids had lost. Innocence stolen. Hope shattered. All he could do was kill the monster.

A half an hour later, Asher parked blocks away from the foster home and set out on foot through the woods that Maxwell had walked him through last night. He'd taken note of every step. The whole time Maxwell chatted away, Asher wrote out his murder in his mind.

1. Come to the foster home through the woods. There's no cameras nor security.

2. Kill him in the office. Make him scream.

3. Change right there.
4. Leave back out by the woods.

Asher weaved between the trees. A good wind had picked up and washed the yachting accident's stink off the island. More people traveled around Ovid today. He'd passed tons of people on his bike, with his helmet sitting firmly on his head and hiding his face. Some seafood festival was going on around the northern tip. Traffic went in that direction—a long road of Bugattis, Porches, and new Rolls-Royces. The foster home staff had probably taken the kids to the festival. The island didn't provide many childrens activities so events like that were flooded with nannies running after little ones.

The more Asher thought about it – the more he decided this was a terrible place to raise a child. It was a despicable city to deposit orphans that already had no family. But to leave them on an island with monsters like Maxwell? To have them grow up knowing they'll most likely account for nothing, simply because they were born poor?

Asher wished that wasn't the reality, but it was.

He crept through the woods, got to the back entrance, and used his lock pick to work the back door. In seconds, the knob turned with a gentle click. Breaking in was necessary. With places like this, most didn't bother the kneeling cable guy in the hallway that looked to be doing his job.

How else would he have gotten in, if not that someone had walked him through?

Adrenaline pumped through his veins. He remembered all

the details from Maxwell's tour last night, knew the location of his office, although for some reason Maxwell hadn't wanted to take Asher inside. Later, Asher figured the reason out from Diana.

Asher stared at the door decorated in Maxwell's name, and knocked.

You'll get some extra pain, since you sicked your psycho assistant on my Diana. I should kill her too... even though Diana said no.

He placed the gloves on his hand and readied the bow, keeping it in one hand somewhat to his side. This was the moment he hated the most, the traveling to the victim with the bow and arrow out.

If anyone else but Maxwell opened the door, they'd have to die. This time wasn't like the others. He couldn't let people go anymore. Too many depended on him to be careful— Diana and Flame being the first to pop into his mind.

Please, let it be Maxwell.

God answered his prayers. Maxwell's face appeared as he opened his office door. "Theresa, where the hell have you been? Wait, you're not, Theresa."

"No, I'm not." Asher punched him in the face, slipped into the office, slammed the door behind him, and crashed his fist into his jaw again.

"Ah!" Maxwell's face was glass, and Asher's hand, a slab of concrete. Maxwell fell to the floor like a shattered bowl that would never be glued back together again.

The broken man touched the blood dripping out of his

nose and looked at the red liquid on his fingers. "Who the hell are you?"

Asher locked the door. "I'm a bad guy."

Maxwell shrieked when Asher stepped toward him.

Maxwell's finger shook as he pointed it. "You're going to be a bad guy locked up in jail if you touch me again."

"And who's going to catch me?" Within seconds, Asher got the bow and arrow in position and targeted Maxwell's chest.

"No. No. No." Fear blared in Maxwell's eyes, as the reality of the situation must've hit his brain. "No. I-I didn't do anything wrong. This can't be—"

"Do what I say and I won't kill you right now."

"Yes! Of course! Whatever you want." Maxwell raised his hands in the air. "Anything."

"Take off your clothes."

Maxwell's mouth dropped open. "My clothes?"

Asher pointed the arrow at the palm of Maxwell's right hand and released. It sliced through the air, faster than he could blink. The sharp tip met soft flesh. It pierced through blood and veins. Plastered the hand to the floor just like a thumb tack would hold a piece of paper to a cork board.

"Any more questions?" Asher asked.

"Oh God! Please! Oh God. It hurts. It burns." Maxwell fumbled with his free hand to open his pants buckle, but was failing miserably. "Please. My hand. Oh God."

Chuckling to himself, Asher pulled out another arrow from his backpack. "I bet you're wishing that you hadn't made the office sound proof, right?"

"I-I... " Maxwell shook as he pushed his pants down. Every few seconds, he glanced back at the arrow keeping his right hand to the floor. "I-I... "

"You-You what?" Asher pointed the target at Maxwell's forehead.

Gasping, the man stumbled through his words. "I didn't... make the office... sound proof."

"Yet, you love it just the same."

"I don't understand."

"Oh, the kids would."

"Don't you hurt my kids! Take me instead."

"Finally, something we agree on."

"Don't you touch them!" Maxwell shoved his pants down to his knees and exposed blue boxers with yellow smiley faces painted on the front.

"I should kill you just for those boxers alone. Is that what greets the kids' eyes right before you stuff your nasty dick into their little mouths?" Asher pointed the arrow at Maxwell's forehead.

"I never!"

"Never?"

"Never! I would never. I've never, ever touched my kids." Tears spilled from Maxwell's eyes. "All my life, I've protected them and others. You don't understand—"

"Take your dick out."

"Please," Maxwell whined. "Please. Please. Don't hurt me. I'm so scared."

"You should be."

"I'm so scared."

"I'm sure the kids were too."

"I didn't." Spasms quaked through the man. Spit flew out of his mouth. Out of all the others Asher had killed, this man had no dignity what so ever.

"Take your dick out," Asher growled.

Maxwell pulled the flimsy thing out of the hole of his smiley face boxers, his fingers shaking with the movement. It lay there.

"How many kids have seen this?" Asher asked.

"None. Never. No one. I swear."

"How many kids without a caring parent to love them, have come to this facility with hope, and you've fucked the glory of life right out of their little bodies?" Rage roared in Asher. "How many!?"

"None!"

"How many!?"

"None. I swear."

Asher targeted Maxwell's dick and released the bow. The pointed-tip slammed into the shaft with a boom, and kept that body part to the floor. Maxwell was now nailed to the ground by his hand and dick, there'd be no more running.

No more chances for him to get out of this.

"Too bad," Asher said. "I wish I had a number. Now, when I cut you, I'll have to guess the amount of kids you've injured, and just carve it in that way."

Maxwell no longer spoke. He just shook and groveled, his

gaze locked on the green and dark brown liquids spilling around the arrow and his penis.

Interesting. I should study anatomy way more than I do. Those are beautiful colors right there.

Asher kneeled and gazed at the punctured penis, studied the torn flesh that surrounded the arrow's length like a sick blooming flower.

Asher breathed in the scents around him—blood, urine, and something else.

Aww. Fear. Yes. It's been a minute since I've smelled good old-fashioned fear. I should've brought Diana here. Would she have loved to see this? Definitely.

Maxwell mumbled words to himself, "God take me into your gates and bless me. I've done my best t-to live your way. I-I've—"

"Shut up. Before I cut your tongue next."

Tears streaked down Maxwell's reddening face. Snot dripped in green goop from one nostril. "I swear. Please. Please. Don't kill me. I'm scared to die. I don't know what's on the other side."

"Don't you know? It's your God that you've just been praying to."

"Is he really there?"

"Him or her. Yes."

"Will this God take me?"

Asher positioned the third arrow and pointed it at Maxwell's chest. "No. That God won't take you, but someone else will."

The arrow flew through the air and buried into Maxwell's chest. He crashed into the floor, screaming.

"Don't worry. I made sure not to get your heart. We've only just begun. No need to rush." Asher dropped his bow and arrow, took out his knife, and walked over to his victim. "So you asked me a question. Will your God take you? No, I say. Never. Not a sick man like you."

"I-I didn't touch the kids. I-I—"

"However, there is a comforting alternative. You have a new master. A grotesque one on hooves, but one nonetheless. This God lives far below. He waits behind the gates of hell, rubbing his horned cock and spilling his sperm into flames."

"P-please just kill me now. I can't take this."

"Have you ever dreamed of fucking a devil?"

The man shook his head no and cried some more when he spotted the knife in Asher's hands.

"Oh, goodie. Then you're in for a surprise. That's what you deserve, to be bent over and slammed into raw." Asher caressed Maxwell's chin with the blade, one long swipe. "Satan loves me too. It's an odd relationship. I send him things every month, although I don't serve him. I send him back his monsters. He loves those presents."

"I'm not a monster. I swear."

Asher knew he shouldn't have, but he did it anyway. With his finger, he dabbed at Maxwell's tears and tasted them. Salty liquid greeted his tongue. A shudder ran through him.

All Maxwell could do was scream over and over.

Asher put one finger to Maxwell's lips. "Shhh.

Remember, no one can hear, but me. And you don't want to annoy me. Although you're going to die in lots of pain, I do try to keep it somewhat humane. But if you force my hand with annoyance," he leaned in closer and whispered into Maxwell's ears, "I'll fucking make you bellow like a pig while you watch all of your body parts in a pile in front of you. There are ways to keep you alive enough to see your legs get separated from your body, inch by inch."

Maxwell cringed and shut his eyes.

Asher cleared his throat. "Now what was I saying. Oh yeah. Right now, I'm going to wrap you up, really well, and send you along to your new God. Too bad all of those kids you hurt couldn't have been here to see it."

And so, Asher began his dance.

Although the arrow was fun, nothing gave Asher more pleasure than a nice carving of flesh. A blade melting through skin, stained with a red tint. It could've been the closeness that was necessary with a knife.

Stabbing a person was intimate, erotic in the cruelest way.

Each time, Asher thrust the blade into Maxwell's shivering flesh, Asher's cock hardened just a little bit more.

He pounded that blade into the man's gut. Warm blood spurted onto his gloves. A sloshing sound filled the air, it reminded him of the sex with Diana the night before. How wet and gushy she'd been? How lovely his cock dripped with her?

God, I wish I could take these gloves off and stick my hand in his stomach. I bet it's as warm as my Diana's pussy.

Maxwell whimpered.

Asher laughed. "If you only knew what I was thinking, you'd probably cry out louder."

Asher did his job with skill, flayed the man hard with his knife.

He hammered it into him,
quickly,
with no grace,
just desire to bring more pain.

Boom.
Boom.

Over and over.

Bits of skin flew in the air like flakes flew when one picked ice. The body jumped with each impact, each greeting of flesh and knife. A few times, the sharp tip hit bone and scraping sounds ensued. It gave him a new idea, so Asher drew zig zags into the bone's white hardness.

Let the police figure out what the Cupid is trying to say.

I can hear them now. "These carvings in the bone could be tribal?"

"No, it's a sadistic ritual."

"Wait, maybe it's a hidden message."

By now, nothing was left of Maxwell.

Only God knew when the man had died.

Asher had begun with Maxwell's stomach and then poked holes all down his legs. Torn flesh dotted each thigh. All of his toes sat across from his feet. His arms hung loose and had a checkered pattern down to his elbows.

His face looked like a fresh pound of slaughtered meat, just butchered and newly ground, and sitting on the floor away from his body, just waiting to be cooked.

He gazed at his work and smiled.

Should I leave another message? Sure.

He walked over to Maxwell's desk and wrote in blood, "Cupid was here."

CHAPTER TWELVE

DIANA

In her dream, Diana rode Asher's thick cock like a good girl, bouncing up and down on that lovely length that had brought her so much joy. Their reflections danced back in the mirror.

It was such a weird room. A king-sized bed sat in the center of darkness. They were on it, humping hard, making the mattress shake, the box springs creak. Heat swarmed around their sweaty skin.

Breathless, she picked up her speed, her full breasts bouncing. Asher kept his face near them and lapped at her nipples each time they came close to his tongue.

"Yeah. Give me that pussy!" With both hands he gripped her ass and rammed her down on him harder and harder.

"Wait," she gasped. "Slow down."

"I love it. I love it."

"Asher? Slow down."

He slammed her on him even more, her folds swelling in pain and desire all at the same time. Her head flopped back and forth in the erratic rhythm.

But... oh... oh...

Even with the ache, an orgasm bloomed in her core.

"Take it!" Asher roared.

"Ah!" Pleasure swallowed her body, washing through every inch of her body.

Dizzy, she turned to the mirror and froze as terror stared back at her.

Instead of Asher and her reflections, there was death. It should've been two lush bodies grinding against each other.

No.

It was worse.

The reflection displayed two pumping corpses. Two love consumed monsters. Gray flesh decorated both of their bodies. Their faces were just scared and worn skulls. On Diana's mirror creature, a few black strands hung to her shoulders. Tufts of blond hair scattered across Asher's dead body.

"The mirror..." Diana blinked and tried to stop Asher.

Growling, he pulled out of her, picked Diana up, and put her on her back. "Touch your toes, Diana."

"No." She tried to catch her breath. "Look in the mirror. Something is wrong."

Fear pumped in her chest.

"Oh my little cat. Are we not curious?" Asher asked with a grin. He clutched her breasts, squeezing. "Touch your toes, darling."

She sat up, frantically looking from side to side. "Asher,

something is wrong. I don't understand."

Her voice echoed into the darkness.

"I don't understand."

"I don't understand."

Kids appeared and then laughed right next to her.

"What the hell?"

The girls sang a song, or maybe it was a riddle? Two little girls with red pig tails, jumped rope right next to the bed.

"Fuck me," the girls sang as they jumped the rope. "Fuck me hard, Cupid. Make me bleed."

Bile rose in her throat. "No! Stop saying that. No!"

Diana turned to the mirror, and although the real Diana and Asher stopped having sex, the corpse depictions of them continued to make love. Dust crumbled onto the bed within the mirror. Spider webs draped their ankles and elbows. Jagged groans fled their cracked lips. Roaches crawled over her reflection's rotting nipples, and Diana swore she felt the creepy things on her own body.

"No!" She batted at her actual breasts, but nothing was there.

"Touch your toes, Diana," Asher said again.

"Look." Diana tapped Asher several times and pointed to the mirror. "Something is wrong with our reflections."

"You're just so curious. Don't look that way."

"I can't," Diana countered.

Asher snorted and gestured to both of them. "The mirror shows what it wants to show. This right here. The powerful thing living between us. That is the only thing we should focus on."

"But the mirror—"

"Ignore it."

"I can't!" Diana screamed.

"Fuck me," the girls giggled and sped up their jump roping. *"Fuck me hard, Cupid."*

"Stop saying that!" Diana screamed. "It's wrong. It's so wrong."

"Oh Cupid! Fuck me! Fuck me!"

Diana turned her attention back to Asher and begged, "Get these little girls out of here and make them stop. This is wrong."

"Or is it right?" Asher held his cock in his hands, and then let go. "Don't think about those girls or even the mirror. Just. Touch. Those. Toes."

"Oh, fuck me, Cupid!"

"Everyone, shut up!" Diana held her hands to her ears.

"Fine." Asher released his cock and crossed his arms around his shoulders. "I'll be quiet and look into your mirror."

Diana opened her mouth in shock. The girls and jump rope disappeared. Light appeared above them and bathed the mirror's surface in a white glow.

"I hate looking at this." Asher faced the mirror.

Diana slowly rose to stand next to him. "Why?"

"Because it always shows me the truth." He spit on the ground next to him, and they stood their together, watching the rotting corpses making love.

In Asher's bedroom, Diana woke up in darkness, drenched in sweat. Silk sheets stuck to her skin. Her hair lay all over her head. Her heart boomed in her chest so loud she couldn't hear anything else. Asher's last words from the dream rang loud in her head.

"Because it always shows me the truth."

"Jesus!" She jumped out of bed and touched her body, every inch, scared that the roaches were still crawling all over her. "What the hell was that?"

Her throat was raw and the skin beneath her eyes stiffened with dried tears. Dreams like that tended to gnaw at the day. She knew she'd think about the details all morning, and continue to ponder them by the afternoon. Once the evening came, she'd be nervous about closing her eyes and falling back to sleep.

"Dreams reveal truths." Her grandmother would pat her head and hug her tight, before sending a little Diana right back to bed when she was younger. "Don't you ever forget that, girl. Dreams say the things that the heart won't listen to, and the brain is too hard-headed to grasp."

Since she'd discovered Asher was Cupid, her worlds of slumber had shifted to dark and dreary landscapes full of disturbing things.

What is my heart trying to tell me? Oh what am I even

saying? Now is not the time to worry about dreams.

Yet, common sense tugged at the back of her head. Her dreams weren't reality, and she didn't possess any supernatural powers where she fell asleep and saw things in the future. No. She had no talent for sorcery.

However, Diana never ignored her dreams. They'd gotten her out of some pretty difficult spots.

They'd also gotten her in trouble too.

At ten years old, Diana fell asleep and in the dream chased a copper-colored pixie out into her backyard.

"Dig," the pixie had begged, while glitter spilled from the sides of her lips. "Dig and you will find your future."

The next morning, Diana did as the pixie ordered. She dug all day, but it wasn't her future in front of her. Instead, Diana discovered her babysitter's dead body.

That dirty space behind her house had always been her favorite place to dig. Somehow, the dirt stayed cooled during the hot summers. In winter, snowmen sat ontop wooden horses, embarked on noble adventures, and scaled ice castles just like the great Don Quixote. She'd read that novel so many times in that same patch of yard. Who couldn't love a man who consumed so many chivalrous novels that he lost all of his sanity and set out on a quest to undo the injustices of the world?

The pixie had said, "Dig and you will find your future."

In the end, had the creature been right or wrong? Did any of it even matter? Diana the child, had believed that she'd discover treasure. Instead, she found a dead body. Hadn't

Diana been digging up dead bodies the rest of her life, in some way or the other?

And her yard.

Had it just been a regular place? Maybe, she would've never dug up the dead body in the first place? Maybe it was all some odd coincidence that a pixie would come to her and then the next thing, such a strange thing occurred.

She never told a soul about the dream. Everyone always knew that she found her babysitter, but no one knew about the dream.

But that patch of land. That dirty space behind her house. For some reason Gabby's killer had chosen to dump the teenaged babysitter there. It had always been a great place to dig. People dropped loose change. Diana had found other treasures too—long gemmed earrings, tattered pages from porn mags, and two turquoise rocks that glinted under the sun.

Due to a dream, she dug more than she ever would have.

For hours, Diana shoveled, broke the soil, lifted it up, slung it to the side, and started all over again. Never stopping. Never getting sidetracked. She just shoveled and did so some more.

By the afternoon, she saw something that froze her stiff. A gray hand greeted her eyes. Copper rings sat on three fingers, reminding Diana of Gabby's jewelry.

"Dig and you will find your future."

Upon spotting Gabby's corpse, Diana didn't alert her parents—two people that had been fighting all morning over her father's recent lack of work. Diana didn't tell a neighbor or go grab a friend. Her being the odd girl in most situations, it never gave her much opportunity to ever make friends.

"This must be the future," Diana had thought.

And so, Diana had been the one to find the dead body, so she'd been the one to call the police.

And through tear-blurred eyes, at ten years old, Diana had been the one to watch her father get arrested for Gabby's murder. She'd also been the one to hold her mother as she fell to the ground and cried.

One thing Diana hadn't realized at such a young age was that a dead white girl in a poor, black man's yard, didn't trigger court-approved justice in the eyes of society.

Yet, Diana had been the one to hide the guilt of his death deep inside of her, never allowing it to escape, never washing her hands of her father's blood.

A week later, the police found Gabby's actual killer three houses down from Diana's home. And she never saw the copper pixie again.

The first summer after her dad's murder, Diana stayed in South Carolina with her grandmother.

And the odd dreams returned. One night she swam in a dark world with bloody water. The next day, she saved her grandmother's drowning black kitten. Granted, the little furry creature hung around the pond behind the house, every day, and didn't look like he could swim at all. It would've only been a matter of time before the poor thing crept along the branches near the pond, and fell in.

"No, girl. Always listen to your dreams," Her grandmother had said the day she saved her cat.

Perhaps that's when she had transformed into her very own version of the kitten. A curious, black cat.

Whenever Diana scraped her knee, her grandmother would always rub the dirt away from her legs, hold Diana tight in her arms and whisper, "What don't kill a child, makes that little one stronger. And you girl are a mountain, so high I know you can see God's glory high above the clouds, and so strong, there ain't nothing that's going to knock my baby down."

It was like the dreams and her grandmother were trying to prepare her for something more. Every time the kind woman declared Diana's strength, a brick thickened within Diana's flesh, fire heated her blood and roared in her ears. She would curl those little fingers and bite away the pain of her father's death and all the wrongs of the world—racist police officers and dead babysitters.

And so, Diana grew into a mad woman, obsessed with bringing justice into society, but never truly seeing the reality of the world around her.

What was this dream trying to tell me? Two rotting corpses humping each other in the mirror? Is that really us? Or is that just what my heart sees? And what about those little girls saying all of those nasty things?

Diana ran her fingers through her hair as if she could comb all of the craziness out of her mind, just by touching her head.

Forget about the dream.

"Asher?" She looked around the empty room, found her robe, got up, and put it on. "Asher?"

Where did he go?

Still feeling a bit exhausted, Diana went into the bathroom and stood in there for a few seconds, taking the décor all in. This was the first time she'd actually taken the time to study Asher's style. All the other days she'd been either so overcome with curiosity of Cupid or fear of Asher.

White paint covered the walls. The bathroom's space was the size of a master bedroom. A huge hot tub sat in the center with marble steps and gold fixtures. A big shower stood on the side. His and her sinks lay opposite. Around the back was a vanity table with shelves full of toiletries. Other than that, nothing else stood out. There was nothing personal in his space that said, Asher. Not any little funny photos or notes, neither a cherished saying near the vanity table or a quirky framed picture above the toilet.

Just white, gold emptiness.

I wonder if he feels alone in here. Hell, I wonder if he feels alone all over this huge mansion.

She entered the shower, not sure if she had the time in the day to just sit back in a hot tub and pretend everything was alright.

I have to clean up, find Asher, and figure out what's going to happen next.

Warm water poured down over her head, drenching her hair and streaming down her skin. *Perfect.* For those few minutes, she could pretend that everything was normal, that the relaxing moment of water slipping against flesh was the most exciting thing that would happen that evening.

Months ago that was her life. She woke up in the morning, masturbated in the shower, ate breakfast, went into work, read a book, did research, wrote until her fingers numbed, returned home, ate dinner, and then masturbated in the shower. That was her life every day. It began and ended with the same outcomes. Boredom and this sense of hunger for something more filling her chest.

Since Asher had entered her life, the shower was the only moment in the day where she could catch her breath, and there was no need for masturbation, with the way he imprinted himself onto her each time.

Asher filled her day with fear and tossed in surprises in the evenings. He was a sick magician. Tricks escaped from under his wicked sleeves, and she sat there clapping like a dreamy audience. There was no doubt that every future day would keep her heart pumping blood erratically. Everything about him intrigued her—those piercing eyes and wicked past, his hunger for vengeance and his chivalrous need to protect her.

Most of the time she shivered in both fear and lust.

When his gaze hit her, a rush ran through her—she had to blink through the sensations, wiggle her toes to keep her balance, and close her fingers in and out just to make sure she hadn't been transported to another realm somewhere off in the universe where a relationship with Cupid could work out in a happy ending.

What happened? Yesterday, I sat in his bed frozen and scared, now I'm... in love or walking toward that way, and wondering how we... or rather... he is going to handle Maxwell. Wondering how long I have to wait to see him again.

Wait. Am I...
Yes.
I think I might be...

There was no more denying it. And she didn't give a rat's ass what people thought. Lust and love and fear and hope have no time limits. She may have lost Neil just a few weeks ago, but he'd been dead to her for years. She'd already buried the part of him that she once loved the fifth time she saw him fucking their real estate agent on the granite countertop of their new home. The one they were supposed to share together. In joyous matrimony.

Joyous, my ass.

People get off on judging—she was guilty of it herself—but no one can predict how or when they fall. She was certain of that now. She was falling in love with him. So much had happened, and somehow it all had accelerated the intimacy between them.

I'm falling for him.

In the shower, she hugged herself. Warm water continued to swarm all over her skin.

I can't see myself without him.

What would that mean for their future? She closed her eyes, leaned back into the glass wall, and let her body fall deep into the hot shower. Steam rose all around her and fogged the bathroom.

Her dream flashed in her head—dying lovers on a bed. They could care less about the spiders and roaches all on them. They paid no mind to the nasty-mouthed girls. All the corpses yearned to do was make love. It was like they were lost, but not yet dead. Rotting, yet alive, they fed off of the passion pushing out of their mouths.

Are we really those two sex-crazed corpses?

A click sounded in the bathroom. Diana opened her eyes, right as the shower door slid open and a nude Asher stepped in.

Steam rose around his nakedness. Fog slid along chiseled muscles and blurred out the view of her sexy god.

Asher served as a dream himself.

A dark and lush one.

The image of him staring at her in the shower all could have been another lovely dream. Steam swarmed around him. Hot water sprayed on his skin as well as hers. He hadn't even said one word yet, but her body woke up—her nipples stiffened, cunt moistened, legs vibrated just knowing that they'd be caressed with skilled fingers.

God.

He could've been another dream,

and Diana would have closed her eyes, let her head fall back, and do anything that this dream man desired.

But it wasn't a dream,
because all over Asher's fingers,
blood dripped.

Its haunting scent pushed out the beauty of the moment.

Asher said nothing, washing it all away from his hands, and whistled some slow song.

It took her several minutes to find her voice as he rid himself of the evidence from whatever he'd done.

She cleared her throat. "Who's... blood is that?"

A smile spread across his face. "Maxwell's. I did what you asked."

"What?" She touched the center of her wet chest. "What I asked?"

"You told me to kill him."

"I..."

"I did what you asked me to. I made sure he wouldn't hurt anybody else." Asher took her into his huge arms, and snatched whatever she was going to say.

His tongue explored her mouth, as his hands did what they'd been born to do. They made her wild, yanked Diana's logic away and then shoved her back into that blurry existence of Asher's world, one full of gray.

Staring into her eyes, he lifted her up, wrapped her legs around his waist, and entered her ever so gently, "I love you, and I will always kill for you."

And then he ravished her until her body ached, her throat ran sore and dry, and there was no other working limb on her body.

Instead of getting dressed, they dove back into Asher's bed. He requested the maid to cook them up a delicious brunch.

By the time the servant came with their tray, Asher's snores filled the room, and Diana stared in the mirror across from their bed, wondering if her flesh was graying and mummifying for real or if that was just her future laid out in front of her like a bad omen.

CHAPTER THIRTEEN

ASHER

The next days after Maxwell's death were the best moments of Asher's life.

In his bedroom, magic appeared in the most unusual places. Life shimmered in the sunlight as it bathed his and Diana's naked bodies, moving together in only the silence of their moans and the noise of skin slapping together.

Love flowed in that space.

It bloomed around them,
in every second he gazed into her eyes and whispered, he loved her,
in the times he lifted her chin and tasted her lips.

Lust didn't feel like that, an undying need to just wrap oneself into another and shut the whole world out.

Asher belonged to Diana,
like a plane crashing into the hard cliffs of a mountain,

there was no hope,
no sense of escape,
just the rules of gravity,
the weight of love,
dragging them down in a dark abyss.
Magic bled into that room.

Diana fascinated him. They talked for hours, snacking whenever a servant brought their favorite treats. They argued about politics, reminisced about their shared loved for old music groups, and quizzed each other on the lines of their favorite childhood TV shows.

A bridge of intimacy began to build between them,
something thick,
and uncrushable.

Something incredibly different than sweat and sex and pleasure.

There's something to be said for the way a woman's smile can pierce through the skin and touch bone. And to never have to wonder if their conversations would lull or fall below superior intelligence. Her brain made Asher hard.

Wonder leaped from Diana's tongue as she told him about her childhood—mysteries and dead bodies in a back yard, dreams that foretold impossible things and a little girl who dealt with the guilt of having a hand in her father's murder.

That's something we have in common. We both killed our

fathers. Though mine deserved it, and hers came from the injustice of a broken world. We're both trying to fix this world too. We bleed the same desires.

He told her about his mother, the truth, things he'd never said out loud in his life. Her ears took in things that he'd sworn to himself that he would take to the grave.

In days, she'd earned his trust, fully, completely and without doubt. He wasn't sure when it happened—just that it did.

It felt like the weight of the world had been tossed off of his shoulders and he was... free.

Diana did that when no one else could.

Outside his estates, the Ovid Island police had discovered Maxwell's tortured body and the message that Cupid had been there. More helicopters rose from the island, more bad guys fled. No one walked the streets anymore. The shopping district was a ghost town from a horror movie. Restaurants closed early. Less servants traveled to the island.

Asher kept all of these things from Diana, made sure the servants never brought up the newspaper that Diana continued to inquire about.

Flame texted him any new updates when needed.

He kept the outside world out, so he could keep Diana in.

He focused all of his energy on Diana.

On the third day, he rented a yacht and had a staff take them to Key West.

More Miami Dade County cops filled the island. Things were heating up, lots of questions were being asked.

"Have you ever been to Key West?" He wrapped his arms around Diana as they stood on the yacht's deck and watched the waves crash away into more waves.

The keys ran on their right, bridges rose from the ocean like monuments of history. Those structures had been there for years, connecting each key together and gluing themselves to Florida.

"I've been there once." Diana rubbed his arm as he held her.

The salty breeze whipped through her hair and the thin cotton sundress she'd worn that day. The white against her brown skin brightened the glow around her even more, and Asher found himself touching her every second of the day, unable to move away from her rosy scent, that voice, the silk of her skin, and the magic of the garment, hugging her frame.

"Did you hear what I said?" Diana asked.

He blinked and chuckled. "You said you've been to Key West once."

"I said a whole lot after that."

"Like what?"

"What were you thinking about while I was talking?"

"You naked."

She twisted around and faced him, her breasts pressing into his chest.

He groaned.

"I don't believe you," she whispered.

"You don't believe that I was thinking of you without your clothes on?" He winked at her. "You don't know me that well, if you assume my thoughts are more profound when you're around."

"You're worried."

"I'm not."

"Have you heard any news?" she asked.

"Nothing, besides what I've already told you. The police found Maxwell's body. They don't have any suspects for who Cupid could be."

"And that's it?"

"That's it."

"They haven't contacted you?" she asked.

"No, why would they?"

"You could be a suspect. You were at the party. There was an incident where you were around—"

"You've just described me, and twenty other men."

"You were close to the other murders," she argued.

"How?"

She parted her lips and didn't say anything.

"I wasn't any of the men's friends. Any of the guys' events I went to, over half of the island attended also. Half the time, I pretend to be a bumbling drunken idiot with a low IQ and a tragic rich boy with a dead mother." He kissed her. "But let's talk about something else. What did you do, when went to Key West?"

"I don't want to talk about something else. This is important. You could be considered a—"

"This isn't my first murder, Diana. You know this. I've gotten away with many. This is the easiest one to escape. My mother and I were always the first suspects for my stepfathers' murders. Those made me nervous and still I got through it. Maxwell's death is nothing. There's nothing linking me to him."

She bit her bottom lip. Fear hinted at the corner of her eyes, and he immediately regretted reminding her about his bloody past.

Although knowing better, he continued, "Maxwell's death is nothing. There's not one thing that could link me to him."

"You're wrong."

"How?" He raised his eyebrows.

"I'm your link. I could connect you to all of them."

Tension built in his shoulders. "How? You would need more than just saying it. You would need proof."

"I could get it with enough digging."

He gazed off into the ocean. Miles of water extended out. It seemed like a limitless rippling floor, a place where scary things swam below, creatures that humans had never heard of.

He turned back to her. "Why are you talking like this?"

"You're not taking this serious."

"No, that's not an answer." He tucked a few black strands behind her ear. "Why are you threatening me?"

"I'm not."

He let his fingers linger along her neck for a few seconds, before pulling away. "Threatening me is very dangerous."

"I need you to take me seriously."

"I do."

"No, you're not." She poked her finger at his chest. "You're hiding things from me. For some reason, you keep me away from the local news and even newspapers."

"I do not."

"You're lying." She poked him hard.

He jumped. "Okay. I'm lying a little."

"What are you hiding?"

"Nothing really."

Diana tilted her head to the side. Even in the short amount of time they'd spent together, she had learned his expressions. The slight inflections of his voice. The nuances of his body language.

"Asher..."

He smiled. "Okay, my curious cat. Here's the deal. The police have come to the same conclusion you have: Cupid is killing supposedly bad men. They originally thought it was a low-life with a vengeance but now they think it might be someone better at hiding."

"So things are serious?"

"No."

"Then why did you hide it?"

"Because I didn't want you to worry and think things are bigger than they are."

"Bullshit," she hissed.

The yacht continued to slice through the ocean, traveling toward the most southern tip of Florida. The trip had been a way for them to further enjoy their lives and forget the horrors of Ovid Island.

"Let's move on," he said. "What did you do, when you came to Key West?"

"If there are more police on the island, than they are treating this like you're a top serial killer. They may have even linked you to prior murders away from the island."

"Hmmm," Asher said. "Let me guess where you went when you came to Key West."

"You may have to leave the island and go off the grid somewhere."

"You're a writer, so I know that your first stop had to be a tour of Ernest Hemmingway's' house. It's a big thing down there, and for a writer, it's probably like Christians going on a walk to Mecca."

She shook her head. "You're talking about Islam. Muslims do the pilgrimage to Mecca, and yes, I went to Ernest Hemmingway's house. But none of that matters because right now I need to understand what's next."

"What's next?" Asher shrugged. "What's next is Key West."

"And after Key West?"

"Paris or New York, Australia or my bedroom on Ovid Island. Any damn place you want to go, I'll take you, and we'll stay as long as you like, and I'll make love to you as many times as you need, and you'll never have to worry about a thing, besides where to sit, while I take care of it all."

She opened her mouth in shock. "That's not what I mean."

"Then what do you need from me?" He ran his fingers

through his hair with both hands, trying his best to rid himself of the rising irritation flowing around him.

"What's next?"

"What do you mean?"

"You murdered Maxwell. Police want answers. Hell, everyone on the island wants answers. Now what?"

He licked his lips. "I make love to you, and learn everything I can about what makes you, you."

"If you get away with these murders, will you kill again?"

"If?" he asked through clenched teeth.

She cleared her throat. "Will you kill again?"

He backed away and dug his closed fists into his pockets. "I don't want to talk about this anymore."

"We need to."

"I know."

"Then, when are we going to talk about you killing, and what... I mean... I don't know. If you kill again... Jesus. Listen to me. I don't know how to do this, Asher. I'm not sure I can be with a murderer.

"Too bad then."

"Huh?" she asked.

"Too bad that you don't have a choice with whether you could be with me or not."

"Now you're threatening me?"

"I'm sorry." He closed the distance between them and held her waist, scared she would tumble over the deck's railing and fall into the wavy waters. "You want answers, and I'm afraid to give them to you."

"Just tell me."

"And what do you think you would do with those answers?" He frowned. "Don't you think it's better for a bird to be trapped in a huge cage where the trees and flowers hide the bars, instead of a tiny one where all the wiring is right there in front of her face?"

"Am I a bird again?"

"You never stopped being my bird."

"I'm your equal."

"No, you're not."

"Excuse me?"

"You're above me, Diana."

She stumbled on her next words. "T-that's... you're trying to get me off track."

"No, I'm telling you the truth." He traced the outline of her lips with his thumb. "You're my bird. You rule me in many ways, but when I lead, you follow, because I know this world, and I just want to keep us protected."

"This is back to kidnapping."

"So then that's what you want to know. What's next?" He shook his head. "Next is not an open door, Diana. Next is not you away from me. Next is not freedom, or anything but my love. You'll be provided for, and given anything you ever desired, from money to your career. You'll write and work where you damn well please. We'll live where you want. We'll do what you need, but next is not going to be you returning to your home. Next is not breaking this off. Next is not you ever being away from me. Next is not..."

Diana's bottom lip quivered. "You're holding me too tight."

He let her go. "I'm sorry."

"This is wrong."

"What is?"

She walked away from him and the deck's ledge. "All of this. You can't just decide that we're together forever. It's not how things are done. I'm not a doll."

"Then how are they done?" He blew out an exasperated breath.

"We date. We get to know each other. We take our time. What we don't do is kill people around the island, and kidnap me in the process."

"And just for discussion's sake, what would we do if, I did?"

"Did what?"

"Kill people around you and then..."

"Kidnap me"

"Yes."

She rolled her eyes. "Then I run."

"But you aren't running." He licked his lips. "You've been doing everything but running."

"I tried... remember."

He rolled his eyes. "You didn't get very far. So tell me, why haven't you tried since then?"

She hesitated and licked her lips before answering. "I've been enjoying myself, and from time to time, forgetting that you're a serial killer."

"I'm not a serial killer."

"You're not a hero."

"You're right. I'm Cupid."

"Stop."

"You named me." He smirked.

"I didn't know I was naming *you*." She walked away.

He rushed and stopped her by grabbing her arm. "Wait. Don't run off mad."

She kept her back to him. "Apparently, I can't run off anywhere."

"Okay, maybe I'm a bit extreme with my courtship."

"You're as gentle as a serial killer."

He growled.

She replied in a bored expression, "You're not a dog."

"I'm not a serial killer either."

"Let's just agree to disagree on that."

He pulled her close to him and whispered in her ear, "How do you want me to court you?"

"I don't know. It's hard to find a happy medium between being scared shitless and wanting you to bury your dick in me."

He laughed at her honesty. "I think I have the second part covered. So please tell me… how do I stop scaring you?"

"By letting me go."

He tightened his grip on her arm. "I can't."

"You have to." She got out of his hold. "Otherwise this relationship, which is already… unstable, well, it will explode on us both, and real quick."

She pushed him away. "You can't just jail me. That's not love. You want to be with me, then respect my privacy and freedom."

"Okay," he blurted out.

"Okay?"

He tasted that word on his tongue again. "Okay."

"I can move back into my apartment without you hovering in the shadows of my balcony?"

"I can't hover?"

She blinked. "Can I leave your mansion?"

"Yes." He gritted his teeth. "But not because I want you to. Only because you're forcing my hand."

Her eyes widened. "So you'll agree to me not being caged?"

"Well, the island is still a place—"

"Asher, I'm a grown woman."

"I know."

"I'm not a bird."

"But—"

"You try to cage me, and you'll end up ruining it all." She moved away from him. "Do you understand what I'm saying to you?"

He stared at the ground. "Yes."

"And your killing—"

"I think we should handle one thing at a time." He lifted his gaze to her and considered tearing away that beautiful sundress. "You want your freedom to feel better about exploring us. I'll do that for you. Maybe, I was a bit extreme.

But this is me trusting you now, to not only keep my identity a secret, but to..."

"What?"

He sighed. "Don't leave me."

Her voice came out in a low whisper. "Asher."

"Please, don't leave me. I don't have anyone else... not anyone that would understand me."

"Your life." She shook her head from side to side as if the movement could help her brain get it together and make sense of things. "I don't know how much I would be able to take."

"Then we'll see. We'll do it like you said, earlier. We'll date. We'll take our time."

"This is crazy."

"I give you freedom." Asher extended his hand for her to shake. "You give me hope."

"What is this, a deal?"

"Yes, I give you freedom. You give me hope. We try, and see what happens, then come together, talk about it, and try again."

"I don't know if this could even work."

"Freedom and hope." He nudged her hand with his fingertips. "And really phenomenal sex. Don't forget that one.

She gave him her hand. "Fine, freedom and hope. And really good sex."

"Let's just see where that takes us for the next couple of weeks."

"And then after that?"

"I don't know, Diana. I've never been in love before." He kissed her. "I've never loved anybody this much." He sucked on her bottom lip and then let it go. "I've never loved anyone the way I love you... not even myself. But there's no one else I would rather sacrifice or compromise for than you."

CHAPTER FOURTEEN

DIANA

They spent the rest of the day in Key West, racing around the tiny streets, snapping pictures of the funny people who strolled down the pavements—people dressed in costumes, others decorated in only body art. There'd been some sort of fantasy festival happening down there that week. The streets had been crowded, and in every hand someone carried a bright colored cup full of something intoxicatingly good.

They visited Ernest Hemingway's house because Asher had never seen it. It was such an elegant place—the famous author's paintings hung on the walls, the small details of architectural beauty that managed to last after his death, and even the secret treasures he'd filled his home with. Everything had been preserved as if he'd just left his place to go on a nice little walk. He'd been an avid collector of Spanish Seventeenth-Century furniture.

All through the house the famous Hemingway six-toed cats yawned, lounged, and prowled about. There were at least twenty of them Diana had counted. Apparently, the author had been given his first six-toed cat by a ship captain. He named her, Snow White. He'd continued to get more of these little creatures, naming them all after famous stars as each one found their home with him.

The writer had an in-ground pool that had been dug out through solid coral. It was twenty-four feet wide and sixty-feet long. The whole time Asher and Diana walked by it, he whispered in Diana's ear on how he wished he could fuck her in that massive pool.

Due to Asher's confession, they'd veered off from the tour group and ducked into the shadows of Hemingway's garden. He fingered her amidst the crimson hibiscus and blushing pink and white bleeding heart flowers that hung low like angels in the sunlight.

Back on the yacht, Diana couldn't deny that she'd needed that break with him, needed that moment to breathe far away from Ovid Island.

Sparkling turquoise waves stretched for miles beyond Diana's vision. They'd traveled around the Keys and made it to the southern west side of Florida to see the sunset. She'd been to the Keys, but she couldn't remember ever seeing the way the sun dripped yellow and orange streaks of glory into the Atlantic Ocean.

She leaned against the yacht railing, the breeze whipping her hair around and stared out into the vast abyss of water.

"Incredible, isn't it?" Asher wrapped his arms around her waist and she felt the heat of his chest through her paper-thin dress.

They stood there in silence, letting the waves, seagulls, and their breaths do the talking.

Diana spun around and nuzzled into Asher's neck. "Did you mean it?"

Asher lifted her chin. "What?"

"Do you love me?"

He swept a black curl away from her hair, only to have it fall right back in place. He kissed her forehead and sighed. "I can't be certain I know what true love is, Diana. I don't know that I'm... capable. But whatever is going on between us is close enough to the love I've always heard described. The love that is preserved in ivory and black ink. So, I say, yes. I love you."

Diana shivered in his arms. Her heart pumping out the rhythm of her spiked desire. There wasn't a single part of Diana that doubted Asher's confession. Whatever he was capable of feeling, he felt it with her.

And despite the dreams,
the murders,
the need for control,
she loved him too.

In a way that she believed mirrored his. She couldn't be sure he had the capacity to love like others. She was, after all, wrapped up in a killer's arms. But that was just it—she didn't want to be anywhere else.

She thought about telling him to forget the deal. That she

didn't need her space. But she refrained.

Being alone for a few weeks... having a chance to breathe her own apartment air and sort out her jumbled feelings—she needed that. Even if her desire told her otherwise.

She leaned up and nibbled on his bottom lip. He pulled her in tighter. As Diana snaked an arm around the back of his neck and then ran her fingers through Asher's blonde curls, he carried her to the deck sofa and laid her down gently.

Lust laced his words. "Have you ever been fucked on top of a yacht?"

"No," she whispered.

"Well there's a first time for everything." He peeled away her clothing, stitch by slow stitch until her chocolate skin shone against the setting sun.

Her voice came out a few octaves lower than normal. "Your turn."

Desire flooded her.

When Asher touched Diana, grazed his fingertips along her smooth skin, the rest of her thoughts dissipated. Vanished as if they never existed.

Asher was an alchemist with his touch, and she was a victim of his chemistry.

She quivered when he blew soft air on her puckered nipple. She ached for him then. She wanted him everywhere. To feel her breasts enveloped by his mouth, his hands tracing circles down her torso, thighs, and ass. She desperately wanted to feel his cock buried in her soft folds and his tongue massaging her clit.

Calm the hell down. I have nothing but time to let Asher explore me. Or do I?

She arched her back as he suckled on her nipple–hard, then soft, with a quick bite.

When he cupped her other breast with his hand, she guided his free hand down to her pussy. Made him insert a digit to see how wet she was for him.

"See what you do to me?" She whispered.

He let out a groan and smashed his lips into hers. "I'll be doing a lot more to you in a minute."

Asher kissed a path from her lips through the valley of her breasts, down her taut belly until he reached the spot above her clit. He gave it one strong lick and looked up at her as if asking for permission.

Diana's pulse quickened and her clit throbbed. She raised her hips, closing the gap between Asher's mouth and her pussy.

"Oh you want this?" He asked pointing to his tongue. "You want me to fuck you with my tongue? Do you want to feel a quake in your bones as I run my tongue over your clit, nice and slow? Would you like me to burrow myself in your sweet, rosy pussy so I can eat you out the way you deserve to —"

"Asher. Just fucking do it already."

"Someone's impatient."

She pushed his head down and nearly passed out with the first dig of his tongue. He spread her open wider, exploring her with gusto. He massaged the rim of her asshole before teasing his finger in and out. The double penetration created a flurry of tingles in the base of Diana's stomach.

She moaned but it came out ragged, her breath catching in her throat. She was already at the edge, but she didn't want to go. Too soon.

Diana pushed Asher off of her and gave him a 'come hither' finger.

He crawled over to her, kissing her neck, earlobe and then her lips.

"I want your dick in my mouth." She looked down at his rock-solid cock. "Right. Now."

His smirk filled Diana with entirely too much desire to wait. She pushed his hands out of the way and pulled his thickness into her mouth. She licked him from base to tip, fast,

fast,

slow,

slow,

until he moaned her name.

She used her hands as a weapon between cradling his balls, tracing lines on the flesh of his inner thighs and alternating the way she sucked him off.

Sex had always been good with Asher, but this? It was explosive. Intense. And they hadn't even gotten to the main event yet.

"Diana stop, I'm close," Asher whispered.

She shook her head.

He lifted her chin up. "Yes. I'm not done with you yet,"

and then he flipped her onto her back, swiftly, as if he'd done it so many times before.

Diana lost a little breath in the quickness, but panted as her chest rose and fell.

Asher assaulted her throat with light, airy breaths. All around her neck he blew softly as she shivered. He moved lower until he had one of her breasts in sight. Tender kisses fell upon her right breast and just as quickly as the tenderness began, Asher turned hungry. Sucking on that nipple, biting playfully.

Dear God. A few more of those and I'll come undone.

He moved to her left breast and she dug her nails into Asher's back, clenching her oncoming orgasm.

"Let it go," Asher said breathlessly into her chest.

"No. I won't come unless you do."

"I think I can arrange that," he said, smiling. And with that, he slid his cock into her throbbing pussy and thrust slowly.

She drew in a sharp breath and cried out when he began to plow into her.

Diana opened her eyes and through her lust-haze she watched Asher's muscles constrict and contract. His blonde tendrils swaying with his thrusts. With his eyes closed, and his peachy skin layered in sweat, he looked like the painted Gods in one of Diana's Mythology textbooks from college. Even if she wasn't filled with crazy feelings for him, she'd never be able to deny his beauty.

He opened his eyes and stared right into hers. "Diana?"

"Yes?"

"Close your eyes. I'm going to fuck you senseless now."

She smiled as her eyes drifted shut.

"Okay," she mumbled and melted into the shocks and tingles coursing through her body as Asher pinned her arms above her head and buried himself deep inside of her. His moans filled her ears and she quivered with numbing muscles.

She felt drowsy.

Fulfilled.

Content.

Maybe the love-making corpses had it right all along.

Diana woke up as the yacht docked in Ovid Island's marina.

Why are we back here?

The sky was a blanket of darkness and stars. She looked around and saw Asher talking to one of his staff.

He met her eye and dismissed the man.

"You're up." Asher walked closer. "We're back at Ovid."

Diana wrapped her arms around herself. The air had gotten unusually chilly. "I thought we were spending a few days at sea?"

Asher shook his head. "I changed my mind. Our little chat has inspired me to do something I'm not sure I should do, but

I'm going to do it anyway."

"What?"

"How serious are you about your freedom?"

"Very serious."

"Could you love me, Diana? Could you accept the man that I really am?"

"You mean... the fact that you kill?"

He grimaced and then nodded.

Diana's eyebrow rose. "What are you planning?"

"After we made love, I realized that if I lost you, it would destroy me. You're perfect. You're nothing like any woman I've met before. You're nothing like my mother. Maybe, she's why I kept that wall up when it came to my heart. Maybe that's why I never got close to anyone. But, you're not like her."

"No, I'm not."

"I want you to be in my life."

"I... I think I want that too."

"Why don't you know now?"

"Because, Asher, so much has happened, and I need time, before making a serious decision about it."

"And with this time, you'll need your freedom?"

"Yes."

"Well, I've been thinking too. The sooner you get your freedom and realize what you're missing—the sooner you'll be back in my arms."

"Back in your arms?"

"Yes, back with me. Clipping a bird's wings does not

mean they won't fly—it just means they will find another way to escape."

"And now I'm a bird again?"

"At least you're not—

"If you say Don Quixote, I swear I will punch you."

Chuckling, Asher leaned down and kissed Diana on the forehead. "You'll always be my bird, Diana."

"A bird with clipped wings?"

Sighing, he kissed her again. "I'll have my driver return you to your apartment in the city. I'll have your belongings brought over tomorrow."

He dropped his head and turned to leave. This was painful. He was using all the strength in his body to fight against what he really wanted to say to her. She knew him too well already to know the difference. He didn't want her to leave. He didn't want to let her go.

She grabbed his arm. "Just like that?"

He ran his thumb down the side of her cheek. "Just like that. You've got your freedom and time to think about whether you truly can be with me. Then come to me, when you're done."

And she let him go.

Being without Asher, it was something she had to do. Otherwise she'd never know for sure if it was love or fear that kept her by his side.

And she so desperately wanted it to be love.

Three days. She'd been in her apartment alone for three whole days and she was consumed. By missing this independent part of her life, missing Asher, but mostly from the shocking details that had been reported in the news.

Theresa, Maxwell's assistant had been given his entire estate in her boss's will. She'd now put up a million dollar reward for any information on Cupid's identity. All of Miami and now the rest of the country had their eyes on Ovid Island and the amazing CNN-coined Valentine Killings.

For hours, she stuffed her mouth with popcorn, sat on the couch, and watched every sordid detail of the prior murders. They'd looked up all the things she'd discovered, and even cited some of her old articles in the news reports.

"What's surprising is that the latest victim does not seem to fit the personality of the other ones." The news correspondent stared into the camera. *"Although Maxwell Grayson had held charity events on Ovid Island for several years. He'd just moved to the island a month ago."*

The correspondent turned to a screen behind her that showed Theresa sitting in a chair with a bow on top of her head. "Today, we have Mr. Grayson's personal assistant here, who'd been managing his foster home for all the years during his absence."

"Wait a minute. Theresa managed the foster home, while Maxwell was away from the island?" Something hard plopped into Diana's gut.

"How close was Mr. Grayson to his foster kids?" the *correspondent asked.*

"He didn't have much time to come visit, and only was able to make some of the charity events." Theresa touched *her bow, froze as if realizing she'd did it on national TV, and then sniffled. "Maxwell... I mea... Mr. Grayson didn't spend much time with the children. Not like I did."*

A chill ran down Diana's back.

Not like you did? How much time did you spend with them?

The memory of that night with Theresa flashed in Diana's mind. The little woman had been skilled with the rope, and had bound Diana to that chair with ease. If she was the one that truly managed the foster home, then she'd probably been the one to get the sound proof walls installed.

"You, yourself, grew up in the Grayson Foster Home?" *the correspondent asked.*

"Yes. I'd been in another home in Miami, called Holy Trinity. It wasn't a good one. Not a good one at all." Theresa *touched the end of her bow and sniffled again. "The Grayson family saved me. They took me out of there, due to several reports of abuse, and quickly opened up a place in their foster home, where I was loved and protected."*

"I'm glad to hear that."

"I don't know why someone would kill Maxwell."

"Do you have any idea who it could be?"

"None. Maxwell wasn't perfect, but he was never worthy

of this monster Cupid's judgments." Theresa wiped at tears that fell from her eyes. "I don't know about his other victims."

Theresa stared into the camera as if targeting me with her sad gaze. "This time, Cupid killed the wrong person."

"What do you mean by that?"

"I think Cupid believes he is saving people." An odd smile widened over her face. "Cupid didn't save anyone this time. If anything, he's made it all worse."

The correspondent raised her eyebrows.

Diana dropped the bag of popcorn and shut the TV off. "What do you mean, you evil bitch? What are you saying? Was it you that hurt those kids or are you trying to lure Cupid into a trap?"

Maybe, we should kill Theresa.

Diana despised the wench, but she also felt sorry for herself, in this sudden realization that the woman and maybe even those foster kids were beyond saving.

Or maybe we are all crazy? Who am I to judge anymore? Everything that I've done so far could put me right into a mental hospital for the rest of my life.

Who kidnaps someone else like she did unless they're crazy? Theresa. Who gnaws on their cheek and bites into flesh? Me. Who carves their name into a dead man's chest? Asher. Who asks another man to kill for her? Me.

Who may ask him to do it again?

Me.

Diana crawled off the couch and lay on the floor. Popcorn

kernels scattered all around her. Since watching the news, she hadn't bathed, changed her clothes, or even slept.

"Cupid didn't save anyone this time. If anything, he's made it all worse."

She was going stir crazy. She thought everything would be better once Maxwell was dead, and she was away from Asher and back in her apartment. Justice would be served, and she'd have her freedom, her familiar closet of designer clothes, and her well-worn but cozy bed in her warm, inviting bedroom.

But none of it mattered.

"Cupid didn't save anyone this time. If anything, he's made it all worse."

It didn't mean a damn thing to her anymore. Not if a pedophile still walked around those foster home walls, spreading disease and horror to little children.

She decided to end it once and for all, really investigate what was going on.

She picked up her phone and called the one officer she'd made friends with at the Ovid Island police station.

Office Slattery.

He'd called her in long ago to question Diana on her husband's murder. She'd met him, and his superior, Captain Rothschild. Both men were so different. The captain had been tall, tanned, and skinny with a neat uniform, and the greed for money in his eyes. Just with one glance, Diana knew that probably half of the millionaires on the island had their wicked fingers in his pockets, filling them up to his desire.

Officer Slattery had been the opposite—pudgy, short, bags under his eyes from probably over-working himself on cases. Food stains and wrinkles decorated his too-tight-for-his-body uniform as if he hadn't enough money to buy new ones.

She'd decided that he could be trusted, and so far she hadn't been wrong.

Picking up the phone, she typed in a message to him.

Diana: *I need your help.*

Office Slattery: *Yes.*

Diana: *I need as much information you can give me on Maxwell Grayson and the Grayson Foster Home.*

The officer was smart. He called, instead of continuing the conversation on text. Something like what she had to say, didn't need to be further recorded in text for lawyers and judges to use against her or him.

She answered on the second ring. "Hello?"

"I can't do that."

"Why not? I thought we had a deal."

"Things are different, since you've been gone." His voice shifted to a whisper. "More cops are here. Federal agents too. Everyone is being watched closely."

"I've been on tons of cases that went that route, and all that my inside people did was print copies of the files."

"I don't know."

"You're on the case, right?"

"Somewhat. I'm more getting everyone coffee and donuts."

"Well, now it's time to do your job. Get me copies of anything on Maxwell and the home."

"Mrs. Carson—"

"Don't you want to be the cop that finds Cupid before anyone else?"

"Yes." Silence passed for a minute, before the officer asked. "Do you have an idea of who Cupid is?"

She swallowed. "I might."

"Hmmm. Who?"

"Just bring it all over." She cleared her throat and hoped she didn't sound desperate. "Please."

"What do you think you'll find?"

"I'm not sure Maxwell Grayson is as innocent as people believe. Someone hurt those kids."

"How?"

"I can't tell you."

"But *you* want me to give you all of my information?"

"Grayson's nurse confessed that she thought he molested those kids."

"Why are you doing this? How is this going to help you find Cupid?"

"I need to know the truth."

"Hasn't the community suffered enough at Cupid's hands? You want to dig up old history and expose the dirty laundry?"

"If the dirty laundry involves kids, yes, I want to air it out for all the world to see."

"That poor man looked like hamburger meat when we came on the scene. Raw and beaten down meat that had been left out for days."

Diana shut her eyes and tried to get that image and Asher's face out of her head.

"Whoever did that is a monster," Officer Slattery said. "He went too far. The federal agents said that they can tell that this guy loves it. Do you hear me? This monster actually is enjoying pounding and flattening human bodies into—"

"I got it, Officer Slattery." Diana dry heaved and held a hand to her mouth.

"We had to find his teeth on the other side of the room, several feet away from his head, just to identify Mr. Grayson's body."

Diana vomited, right there, among the scattered popcorn and old piles of newspapers that had been delivered to her door while she was away. It wasn't long, just a few seconds of brown, buttery fluids leaving her mouth.

The reality bared down on her, and she'd finally lost it.

"Are you sure you're okay?"

She wiped her mouth with her pajama sleeve, got up, and rushed to the bathroom to get towels. "I'm fine. Just fine."

I'm a mess.

"A lot has happened in the last few days and while it's gone on, I've had this terribly bad feeling about you, Diana. Something isn't right."

"Trust me. I was busy." She balanced a pile of towels in

her arms and rushed over to where she'd made the mess. "Will you bring me the files?"

"I'm worried that you'll get hurt."

"I'm fine. Trust me. I'm the last person Cupid would kill."

"How do you know that?"

"I just do. It's my gut feeling."

"I hope your gut feeling is right."

"So… are you going to bring the files over?"

"Yes, Mrs. Carson, but here's my advice, Tread carefully. You know how things work in this town."

"That's the problem," Diana said. "If we'd all be a little more honest and dole out a bit more justice—maybe Cupid wouldn't have to do our jobs for us."

"Maybe, you're right."

They hung up, and Diana spent the rest of the day, trying to get the smell of vomit out of her apartment. By that evening, Officer Slattery had delivered over several boxes of files, and she poured herself into Maxwell Grayson's life.

CHAPTER FIFTEEN

ASHER

Asher: *Anything to report?*

Flame: *A cop came by and delivered about six boxes.*

Asher: *Are you sure it was a cop?*

Flame: *He had the uniform on and everything.*

Asher: *Okay. Thanks. Keep close to her.*

Flame confirmed what Asher had already known. Although Asher had let Diana go back home, he'd also made sure there were several cameras installed throughout the rooms. He kept the bathrooms without them, not wanting to push so much into her privacy.

Drinking and sitting in his private security room, he watched Diana curse out loud, slam a folder onto the coffee table, and pace back and forth.

And then his mother's annoying voice filled the space. "Stop acting like such a pathetic sap, Asher. Really? You're starting to look just like those whipped men who wait on their wives hand and foot. She's just a girl for Christ's sake.

Nothing more. I told you to never get too close to a woman and as soon as I'm gone, you're sniffing between some stupid bitch's thighs like a motherless child in need of healing."

Asher ignored his mother's condescending tone, gripped a glass of bourbon in one hand, and watched the screen some more as Diana paced back and forth in her apartment.

What was going through her head? Do you miss me? Do you care that I'm drinking myself into a stupor knowing I can't be with you? Feel you? Kiss those supple lips, come into your wet, beautiful cunt?

The truth of his decision hit hard. She'd had files and folders on the Cupid case, no doubt, had them delivered as soon as she got back. She was going to dive into working and realize how much she loved it. He was going to lose her.

"It would be for the better, son."

He whipped his head around to see his mother leaning against the wall and sipping a martini.

"Huh?" he asked.

"You're meant to lose her. A woman like that can't stay with a monster like you."

Asher sighed. "You did, Mother. You stayed right by my side."

"Of course. You're my son. I love you by proxy. Not by choice. I'll never leave you like she did."

"Shut up. Just shut up. She will come back. I know it."

His mother slapped the wall with her palms and screamed, "You foolish boy! Do you not see what's in front of your face? You scare her. You sicken her. You make her question everything she believes in. How can you expect her to want to be with you?"

His mother walked toward him and bent down to eye level. Then she got eerily calm and whispered, "You were better off fucking her and then killing her like I told you to do. But no. You never listen to dear old mother."

"Shut up!" Asher dropped the glass of bourbon and cuffed his hands around his mother's neck. For one beautiful second, he could feel his fingers digging into the soft flesh, hear her ragged breaths as he squeezed the life out of her,

but then she was gone.

Just a visceral memory he couldn't ever erase.

The ghost that always kept coming and coming, never shutting up, never giving him any rest.

In the end, all he really choked was air.

Diana will come back to me. I know she will. You can just shut the fuck up, Mother, and stay dead!

Another day passed.

Asher drifted between slumber and the hazy state of his inebriation.

He sat crumpled in his security room. Another drink sat in his hand. He'd stopped counting how many glasses he had, after finishing the second bottle of bourbon. He hadn't slept, just like Diana, who continued to move all over his screen.

Diana remained in her apartment, rushing off to the bathroom and vomiting every now and then.

Is she pregnant or is she that disgusted with the case? Is she looking at pictures of my crime scenes?

All that time had passed, and never had she even considered to text or call. Instead, she did everything else,

reading,

writing,

cursing under her breath,

and pacing.

She was engulfed by something and little bubbles of furious jealousy raged inside of him.

Files, as well as, ink, and paper were stealing Diana away from him, and he would just have to sit back and drink more to get rid of the lingering scent of roses she'd left in her wake.

CHAPTER SIXTEEN

DIANA

After reading thirty-six files filled with summaries on Ovid Island's Foster Home kids, Diana was no closer to figuring out the mystery of Theresa than when she first started. She couldn't find any evidence Theresa even existed. No adoption papers, no court papers. Nothing. Zilch. Like the woman was never there.

Even worse, Diana got to see all of Cupid's crime scenes. They were hard to stare at for more than a few seconds. Blood and torn skin, cracked bones and arrows balanced in empty skulls.

How could I have let him touch me? How could I even feel safe around him? He's not a monster, but he's not normal, either. Focus on Theresa. Focus.

In all of the files, there was no Theresa.

Diana swiped the folder off the counter and screamed as papers fluttered down around her.

She knew Theresa had been there. She recognized the crazed terror in her eyes. So why didn't she have a medical and psych report like all the others? Even the kids that had grown up and left the home had small summaries on them. The police wondered if maybe Cupid was somehow connected to the foster home and had requested everything they could get.

Meanwhile, Theresa continued to crowd all of the news channels. She was the poor mourning friend, crying at the appropriate moments, tugging her bow, and concluding her sad story with the fact that people could send their donations to a special Foster Home PO Box.

Diana planned to visit her psycho friend again, but not until she figured Theresa out. Not until she knew more about what she was dealing with.

If you're involved, then I'll make sure Asher kills you.

"People aren't always who they say they are." Asher had said that to her in bed one night as they laid side-by-side, sweating and panting from their sexual escapades. She'd looked at him and wished it didn't have to be that way.

"People aren't always who they say they are."

And like lightning striking down from the heavens, Diana fell to her knees. She crawled around her kitchen, picking the stray pieces of paper up. She set them on the counter and arranged them back in order.

One by one, she looked through them again. Studied the name and dates and information listed for each child that had a folder.

Okay. Maybe, your name isn't even Theresa. Maybe, it's someone else.

She stopped on Mary Anderson. It wasn't that the little girl was Asian. There'd been other Asian girls that stayed at the foster home until they became adults.

What stopped her was the big polka dot bow on her tiny head. It stared back at Diana from the photo.

How the hell did I miss the damn bow? I need to sleep. I'm missing stuff. Important things.

Mary Anderson had been born on the twenty-fourth of December in Nineteen Seventy Nine in a snowstorm, left to die on the steps of a Catholic church.

Unlike her story on the news, Mary had been sent to Ovid Island Foster Home by Holy Trinity after reports of her "bothering the other kids" and "not understanding the difference between good and bad touch."

By thirteen, Mary was brought up on juvenile charges. Ovid police had caught her with stolen binoculars from the island's hardware store. When they searched for her, she hadn't been there. Hours later, they found her outside of a neighborhood home nearby, watching a mother bath her twins.

Her being a cute girl with a lovely bow, they'd only charged her for the binoculars.

If she'd been a boy, they would've put two and two together and figured she was looking at the naked little kids.

The most interesting piece of paper was a handwritten note on an Ovid Island Police ledger.

Gina Santos, nurse at OIFC called and said one of the

children complained that resident (Mary Anderson)
touched her inappropriately. Sent officer out, but
child denied it. Ms. Anderson denied it also. No
charges or investigation necessary. I am sure this all
was a misunderstanding between two confused little
girls.

Diana felt the first clenching of muscles start in her right shoulder blade.

Stress and anxiety.

The more she thought about the note, the further down the clenching went until her entire body felt rigid. Constrained. Her blood ran cold and she knew right then what the answer was.

Theresa didn't exist because she was really Mary Anderson.

"And Mary has grown up to straight up molestation." Diana hugged the file close to her chest and raced around her apartment.

But did you do this all alone? Did Maxwell know? Was he supposed to die?

She grabbed a coat, her apartment keys and her cell phone. She wished she had a gun or a pocket knife or even Cupid to protect her, but she had to do this alone. She would confront Theresa with the truth and offer her help. And if she refused...

Well then, Diana would call Asher, and leave the woman's life in his deadly hands.

Her phone buzzed right as she took out her keys to lock the door.

She answered, "Hello?"

"Have you found anything?" Officer Slattery asked.

"I think something is up with Theresa."

"The assistant?"

"Yes."

"Funny you should say that. There's been some new developments."

"What?" She paused in the middle of the doorway.

"Maxwell Grayson had hired a private investigator to watch her."

"Do we know why?"

"The investigator hasn't been found. We've been searching for him. He's Miami based."

"Could you let me know what comes out of that immediately?"

He sighed. "Yes, but I think eventually we may need to stop this relationship. I'm getting nervous. This is dangerous for both of us. I could lose my job, and you... you could lose your life."

"No one is killing me. Relax." She stepped outside and locked her door. "Oh, by the way, when did Grayson hire the detective?"

"Around two months ago."

Right around the time he'd gotten rid of the nurse.

"Thanks," Diana mumbled and hung up on Office Slattery.

Outside, a black limo was stationed at the curb. She rolled her eyes. It was one of Asher's no doubt. She walked up to the passenger side window and knocked. When Asher's familiar driver rolled it down, she smiled.

"Did Asher tell you to watch me?" she asked.

"I'm here to drive you around," the old man said.

"I have a car."

"I'll drive behind you."

"That's not necessary."

The man said nothing and stared ahead.

She broke the silence. "Doesn't Asher know how to mind his own business?"

"No, ma'am. He doesn't."

"Well he should learn."

The driver fought against the small smile playing at his lips. "I'll be sure to tell him that ma'am."

"Good. Now, I'm going to leave and I don't want you to follow me. If your boss gets mad, tell him to take it up with me. Tell him I ordered you away."

"I don't take orders from anyone but Mr. Bishop, ma'am."

"There's a first time for everything." She pulled out her phone. "See, here's the thing. I have my bosses' number on speed dial, as well as my own trusted cop. Did you happen to see him come by?"

"Yes, I did."

"I've also left enough evidence up in my apartment for the police to connect the dots on who this Cupid character is.

I don't think Asher would be very happy to find the police at his door, do you?"

The driver stared at her, his almost-smile wiped away by a scowl. "No, ma'am."

"That's what I thought. So who are you going to follow?"

"No one, ma'am."

"Exactly." She raced to her garage where Neil's car sat dormant, backed out of the parking space, and watched in her rearview mirror for Asher's driver to follow. When she saw no one pull behind her, she pressed down on the gas pedal.

She might've liked Cupid for protection, but this was one job she was going to do herself. And after finally seeing photo-by-photo of what the man was capable of, she would have to keep some distance from him, until she absolutely needed saving.

She was going to figure out Theresa's secret, and then she would expose her and Maxwell and the rest of the creepy foster home freaks.

When she arrived at the foster home, it had the aura of being abandoned. Silence permeated the perimeter. Police crime tape waved in the wind. No cars sat in the parking lot, except one, who Diana hoped belonged to Theresa.

This would be her first stop to finding the crazy woman. If Theresa wasn't there, then she'd search until she found her.

Her phone buzzed. Diana checked the screen and read the text.

Asher: *Where did you go?*

Diana: *What happened to you giving me my freedom?*
Asher: *You haven't called or said anything to me since you've left.*
Diana: *I've had a lot to think about.*
Asher: *Like what?*
Diana: *My life.*
Asher: *Not these Cupid killings? I know you're worried about living on the island, but trust me, you'll be safe. I'll do everything in my power to protect you from that mad man.*

She noticed how he mentioned the murders as if he was a regular citizen looking out for her, and not the actual killer himself.

Diana: *I'm not afraid of Cupid.*
Asher: *Trust me. You should be.*
Diana: *Maybe, he should be afraid of me.*
Asher: *Maybe, he is.*
Diana: *I have to go. I'm doing something. I'll talk to you later.*

Dropping her phone back into her pocket book, Diana pushed up the side gate and tip-toed down the path to the foster home's back entrance. CNN had already reported that since Maxwell's death, the kids had been shipped to a temporary living facility in Fort Lauderdale with the hopes that any danger would be gone soon, and they could return to the island.

If someone is here, it's probably her.

She wiggled the knob but it was locked.

Damn. It's too risky to go through the front. But there has to be a spare key. Men like Maxwell were too stupid to think other people would rob what was theirs.

Jumping on tippy toes, Diana rubbed her hand over the door frame but nothing was there. She checked under the flower pot, beneath the grungy welcome mat caked with mud and footprints.

"Dammit!" She aimed a blow to the door. As soon as her skin hit the metal door, she cried out.

Why does that always look easier in the movies?

And then a dark feminine voice sounded behind Diana. "You."

Diana froze and looked back to see Theresa pointing at her, her other hand massaging the bow in her hair. Her cheek was bandaged and taped up, but the reds around the whites of her eyeballs caught Diana off guard.

How crazy was it that Diana hadn't noticed the marks on her face during the news report? The make-up artist must've caked pounds of powder on her face to hide it.

"Theresa... "

"Shut up! Shut up! Shut up!" Theresa yelled and charged at her. She knocked Diana to the ground and pinned her arms down.

"Wait." Diana struggled with her on the ground and shoved her away. "Hey, I came to help."

"Help?" Theresa took one long swallow and then spit in

Diana's face. "You bitch! You ruined everything. You killed him. You killed him."

"I didn't. But he deserved it."

"He did not," Theresa yelled. "How could he? He was a good man!"

Diana looked around her. It was nothing but woods, but she needed to get them both out of there. If Mary/Theresa was in fact guilty, then Diana didn't want to be the last person seen with her.

"Let's go inside," Diana offered. "I can help you find Cupid."

"Maxwell didn't deserve to die."

"He hurt you. That's why you're this way, right? That's why you were so attached to him. Or was it his father or brother? Who did it? Tell me what he did to you, Theresa, and I'll help you. We'll make everything better."

Theresa slapped Diana across the cheek. The tiny woman was stronger than she looked. It came out of nowhere. Diana stumbled back and held in the shock of the pain.

Biting through the hurt, Diana grinned. "Are we not friends now?"

"He never hurt me," Theresa said quietly. "He loved me."

"What do you mean?"

Theresa slung keys at Diana. She caught them, right before Theresa pulled out a gun next, and pointed it at Diana. "Yes, let's go talk somewhere private."

"No one ever told you that guns were dangerous?"

"Guns don't shoot people, people shoot people. And I will

shoot you if you don't unlock the door and go inside."

"Well," Diana cleared her throat. "I won't be sending you a basket of bows for Christmas this year. You can kiss those goodbye."

Diana did as she was told and opened the door.

"Keep your hands up and walk towards Maxwell's office."

I should've told Asher where I was.

Diana kept her hands in the air, while the crazy woman followed behind her. "So you've taken over Maxwell's duties?"

"I've always been in charge of the foster home, since his father died."

"Was his father a nice man?"

"The best. He never touched me."

"Did Maxwell?"

"Yes, but only because I wanted to appear normal. I let him do things to me. But they were by my permission. Anybody that says otherwise should die."

"Well-noted."

They arrived at Maxwell's office. It had yellow crime scene tape crossed in the doorway. Theresa ripped right through it and shoved Diana inside. "Welcome back, Diana."

She groaned. "Not this again."

Although the body had been taken away, death remained. It was faint at first—the coppery, metallic scent, like a penny one sniffed up close. Blood had been spilled, lungs and other things had been punctured, sliced, diced, and skewered.

She'd seen the pictures enough. Lost nights of sleep due to the horrors that Asher's hands could bring.

How could she let him touch her again, she'd wondered? How could she love a monster?

Too bad, she had to face the office where Maxwell had died. It made it hard to ignore the thing that had been ringing in her head all day long.

Vigilante or serial killer, in the end, Asher was a monster.

That morbid truth sank deep into the room's carpet, stained the walls, and lingered throughout the air. Even a stranger could walk in and tell with no problem that someone had died in that room. Terror occurred, and torture too.

And the further into the room Theresa pulled Diana, the heavier the scent of blood became. Like a rotting, rancid stink had burrowed into the walls, the floors. The blood was still there. Over everything. Blood that Cupid—Asher—had spilled, for her.

She bit back the urge to hurl all over the place.

"Do you see this?" Theresa asked.

Diana nodded.

"This is all your fault. You came poking around looking for someone to take the fall for Cupid and you got Maxwell killed! Cupid came for him, instead..."

"Instead of who, Theresa?"

She looked into Diana's eyes and a tear fell from her cheek.

"Me," she whispered. "He was supposed to come for me."

CHAPTER SEVENTEEN

DIANA

"I- I don't understand," Diana said, though she had a bad feeling she did. She wanted Theresa to say it, to make sure she wasn't crazy.

"Maxwell was a good man. He loved me. Like the way a real man should. But... it wasn't enough. It was never going to be enough." Theresa fingered the bow on her head. "I like other things. I like to do things that he would never understand. Have you ever seen how blank and innocent a child's eyes look? It's like—"

"I don't want to hear that. Tell me about Maxwell. Did he ever hurt you? Did his family do something to you, when you were little?"

Theresa's eyes went wide and she slapped Diana across the cheek again. "Of course not. He would never hurt a child."

"Then who did?" Diana touched her face and backed away. "You didn't get this crazy on your own."

Theresa bit her lip and rocked back and forth. "I... I... I

can't tell. I can never tell. He told me to never tell or he'd kill me."

"Theresa, he can't hurt you right now. It's just me here. I won't hurt you. Maxwell is dead."

"Not Maxwell. He would never hurt me."

"Then who?"

She laughed, throwing her head back and varying the speed and intensity of her laughter. "Someone is coming for me. Aren't they?"

"Who?" Diana asked.

"I know you won't tell. But Cupid will be coming." She lifted the gun up in the air, clapped her hands together, and then sang, "He'll be coming round the mountain when he comes... he'll be coming around the mountain when he comes. Oh, he'll be coming round the mountain—"

"Stop!" Diana lunged forward and knocked the gun out of Theresa's hand.

It fell to the floor. A shot rang out. The bullet burst through the wall and left a small hole. Both women turned to the gun and then dove for it. Neither got to it on time. Instead, they wrestled out of each other's grip, each trying to hold the other back as if they could get the gun.

In the end, Diana knew the woman's main weakness.

Diana went for the bow, snatched it away from her head, and jumped to the other side of the room.

"No!" Theresa screamed. "Give it back! Give it back! I can't breathe long without it."

Forgetting all about the gun on the floor, Theresa raised

her hands and shook, staring the whole time at that flimsy bow between Diana's fingers.

"Now tell me the truth, dammit. Tell me who hurt you." Diana wiggled the bow in the air as she hurried over to the gun and picked it up.

"Give it back. Please, I can't breathe." The woman held her hands to her neck and gasped over and over as if she was drowning or choking on water. "I-I can't breathe."

"He'll find me too... he always finds me, when I don't have it on." Theresa checked the window and then grasped more at her neck. "He'll find me and we'll have to play. It doesn't matter how old I am."

"Who Theresa? Who?"

"Reverend Jackson!" She screamed, fell, held her hands to her ears, and writhed on the floor. "Reverend Jackson is coming to get me, and I can't breathe."

There it was. The culprit. It was not Maxwell. He might have been innocent.

A vicious shock went through Diana's spine as she thought about it.

If Maxwell didn't touch those children... then, it must have been...?

"Theresa?"

She didn't answer, just kept shaking.

"Theresa?" Diana asked again and pointed the gun at her.

"I can't breathe. I'm losing my sight. I'm blind. I'm slowly losing my hearing."

"Shut the fuck up!" Diana threw the bow at her and kept

the gun's target on the woman's forehead. "Tell me about Maxwell."

"No, no, no. He'll find me. He'll get me."

"Reverend Jackson?" Diana asked.

Fumbling to put the bow back on her head, Theresa turned and looked at Diana with cold, black eyes. "Cupid."

"Why would he do that?"

Diana closed her eyes, prayed Theresa's answer was different from what she was expecting.

"Because I'm a bad girl," Theresa whispered. "I just wanted them to love me like Reverend Jackson did. I just wanted them to love me. But they didn't! They tried to take my bow. They knew about the power it gave me, so I hurt them. They're all tiny, but I showed those little ones..."

"Stop." Diana's hands shook as she held the gun.

Never in her life had she been so close to killing someone. If the woman described how she'd hurt the kids, she wasn't sure she could stop herself. And would it be wrong? Finally, she'd understood what Asher had been trying to say. Sometimes people had to die. Sometimes one had to take an evil person's life into their own hands, and twist them into nothing.

And poor Maxwell died just because I'd gotten it all wrong. Asher tortured him, turned the man into mincemeat, all based off of the wrong information and my plea to kill him. Now who's playing God?

Guilt rose inside of her chest and corroded any of the goodness that she'd felt that whole year. She'd done the worst thing possible. Once again, like her father, she'd had a hand in killing an innocent man.

Tears slid down Diana's cheeks as she thought of the massacre of Maxwell. She thought of the demand she made to Asher and how he'd followed through. She thought of all those children defiled by Bat-Shit Crazy Theresa who was only bat-shit because someone had stolen her innocence,

erased her youth,

turned her into a psycho pedophile.

Diana couldn't even wipe away the tears. "Maxwell didn't rape those kids, you did."

Theresa nodded and went back to rocking. "And now Cupid is coming."

"You're right. Cupid *is* coming."

Theresa froze and stared her. She didn't even move when Diana took her phone out and dialed.

Asher answered on the second ring.

"Are you okay?" He sounded upset,

or sick,

or maybe even drunk.

"What's wrong, Diana?"

"I'm fine." Just hearing his voice made her shiver in lust, as well as disgust.

What am I going to do about him?

"You need to get to the foster home right now. We have to talk about something."

"The foster home? Diana, what did you do?"

"Just hurry." She hung up on him, and wondered what would happen next.

Should I turn myself in for the part I played with Maxwell? I killed an innocent man. What is going to happen to me? What am I supposed to do? How can I live with it all?

She'd helped kill an innocent man and soon, somehow, she would have to pay for her part in his death.

CHAPTER EIGHTEEN

ASHER

Diana's voice had chilled Asher's blood, cooled the molten lava running through his veins. She was asking for him. With desperation. He thought she wasn't capable of distress, and there it was. She needed him, and he loved the way her voice spun syllables, especially when the words were to summon him.

Asher called his driver. "Do you have an eye on her?"

There was a foreboding silence on the line and then a sigh.

"No, sir."

"What? I told you to—"

"She threatened me, sir. She's a liability."

"She… threatened… you?" Asher asked, though he already knew the answer. Diana was smart and coy and would do what she wanted to get her way. How did he think he could ever protect her, when she was so strong-willed?

But threatening his driver?

"How did she threaten you?" Asher asked.

Flame breathed heavily into the line. "She actually threatened us both."

An uncomfortable sensation stirred inside of him. "How?"

"She said that if I followed her that she would expose us to the cops. That she had a lot of evidence on both of us, and you know that I can't go back to prison."

Asher couldn't help the bubble of laughter that escaped from him. "She wouldn't. She was bluffing, Flame."

"I don't think so."

"Go to the foster home. I'll be there on my bike. Trust me. She won't hurt you or me. She's on our side."

"And if she's not?"

Asher's stomach turned over into itself. "Let me worry about that."

"Yes, sir."

Asher changed into a fresh pair of jeans and a button-down shirt. His hands grazed the top of his bow.

Should I bring it for protection? What's Diana up to? Is she just strolling around the foster home for clues or is this some sort of trap? No. Diana is on my side, not against me.

"At a woman's beck and call. Never thought I'd see the day you took orders from someone… less than you."

Asher spun around and faced his mother. "Funny, I seem to remember taking orders from you, right?"

She reared her hand back and slapped Asher across the cheek.

Of course, it didn't hurt him. She was only a ghost after

all.

"You ungrateful bastard. I only told you what to do to protect us!"

"No. You told me what to do to get rich. To get what you wanted. You taught me to kill innocent men!" Asher lunged for his mother.

She disappeared and left Asher to remember, once again, that she wasn't real.

"I hate you," he whispered.

And a voice sang back from the abyss, "No, Asher, you love me. That's why I'm always with you."

He closed his eyes and willed her voice from his head. When he was sure her memory had passed, he opened his eyes and rushed off to his bike.

The woods surrounding the foster home were silent and the clouds above the treetops were turning a sickly grey. A storm was brewing and it crept into Asher's bones, and made him cold all over.

Something wasn't right.

He hurried through the front doors and down the hallway, surprised to see the yellow crime tape ripped away, as well as the door standing wide open. He approached cautiously.

Screams filtered through the space.

"No! He's going to get me. He's going to be angry. So, so angry. I'm sorry. I'm sorry."

"It's too late for that," Diana said, quietly.

Too late? For what?

"Diana?"

When she looked at him, the desperation in her eyes was so clear. She raced toward him and wrapped her arms around his waist.

"We were wrong, Asher." She sobbed into his chest and when he pulled her away, he tried to wipe the tears from her cheeks, but she shook her head. "We messed up. We have to do something about that. We have to be judged."

Keep her calm. Look into her eyes and make sure she takes her time with her words. She can't ruin all that I've protected.

"Judged?" He intertwined his hand with hers. "Why do we have to be judged?"

"Maxwell. He didn't touch those kids."

Asher chuckled, remembering the sobbing man begging for mercy. "Funny. He said the same thing."

Diana scowled at him. "I'm serious. He never touched them."

"Why do you think that all of a sudden?"

Diana pointed to Theresa. The little woman sat in the corner of the room, rocking back and forth and tugging at a bow on her head.

Women are crazy. They've both lost it.

"This is the assistant." Things weren't making sense to Asher. What was going on and why would she call him here? Was she trying to set him up? Had Flame and his mother been right all along?

"Maxwell didn't touch those kids. In fact, after he let the nurse go, he started an investigation on Theresa. He became suspicious, but was trying to see if it was true. I think he probably would have even done the right thing if given the chance."

Theresa whined in the corner, "Maxwell had an investigator on me? How could he do that?"

"We messed up. Do you hear me?" Diana shook Asher's shoulders, but he barely moved an inch. "We killed the wrong guy. We destroyed another human life based off of bullshit. Because in the end, it was her all along. She's the one who's been hurting them. We're going to be judged. We need to be judged. We killed someone innocent."

She's back in shock. Her mind is twisting and she may never get out of this. She's been around too much death from Neil to Maxwell's photos of corpses. She hasn't slept like me. She... she's not going to make it in my life.

"Asher, why are you looking at me like that?" Diana let go of him.

"How am I looking at you?"

"Like... like you're thinking about killing me?"

"You're being paranoid."

"Am I?"

Again, Theresa whined from the corner, "How could he

put an investigator on me? What was he going to do?"

"Shut up!" Diana screamed, tears spilled from her eyes. "The wrong person died you sick bitch. Shut up!"

Asher rushed to her. "Shh."

He pulled her into his arms and patted the back of her head. "Quiet, my love. It's okay. I'm going to take care of all of this, but this will only work out if you remain calm."

He pulled away and gazed into her eyes. "Breathe in and out slowly."

She looked at him and followed his direction, yet still the tears continued to fall.

"You're not to blame."

"I am."

"I killed him."

"I told you to."

"It wouldn't have mattered, if you told me not to. I would have done it anyway. This is who I am."

"He was innocent."

He cringed, unsure of the truth yet. That was the shit that gnawed at him. That was the thing that bit into his already blackened soul. He'd tortured that man, filleted him because to Asher, Maxwell had been inhuman, nothing but a heartless, soulless pack of flesh that needed to be out of this world.

He'd taken his time because it was his right as a protector of this earth. He'd been proud, and if he discovered that all this time he'd been wrong...

Yes, Diana. We will need to be judged, but only if you can really convince me that this man is innocent.

"How do you know for sure, Diana? Did she confess this to you?"

Diana squeezed his forearm. "Yes, Asher. She told me nasty things. I almost shot her. We were wrong. You killed the wrong person. You're a monster."

You're a monster.

The words wrapped around his bones and squeezed until he felt like he could hardly breathe. The Diana he first met— the one he'd fallen in love with—was not fickle. But the woman standing in front of him... she was weak. She was accusatory. She was... wrong.

Rage darkened his heart. "You told me to kill him."

Diana hung her head and tears dropped to the floor. "I'm sorry. I'm... so, so, sorry. I have blood on my hands, too. This is my fault."

He calmed himself down. "No. Stop saying that. We thought he hurt those children. You and I were just trying to protect them. Sometimes people make mistakes."

Diana sobbed into her hands. "But we were wrong. This was too big of a mistake."

The truth met him dead in the jaw, but still he tried to grasp for something that could take the guilt away. Asher pushed past Diana and grabbed hold of Theresa's shoulders. "Tell me! Tell me she's wrong."

Theresa wriggled beneath his grasp and contorted her face. "You're hurting me. Don't hurt me like this. Hurt me the other way. It's more fun."

Asher scowled at her. "What?"

Theresa pointed to his crotch. "That's the way I like to be hurt."

"Just tell me the truth, dammit. Did Maxwell hurt those kids?"

The woman seemed to fold into herself, her arms wrapping together. "Maxwell was good! Even when I was a bad girl, he was good."

Asher looked to Diana and then crouched to Theresa's level. "You hurt the children?"

She looked into his eyes and all he saw was blankness. A child trapped in a grown woman's body. She nodded her head. "I didn't mean to. It was an accident. They needed to be loved. Pain is love. Pain is love. Pain is—"

"Maxwell gave those kids syphilis," Asher countered.

"No." Theresa smiled. "I gave it to him. He forgave me, but then that nurse found out about the little ones getting infected too. Maxwell didn't say anything to me about it, but I knew he was planning something. It was going to be okay. He'd talked to the police, I think. But it was all going to be okay. But I never thought he would get a detective behind my back. What would he have done to me?"

She gave him the STD, and she gave it to the kids too. She raped them. Maxwell was really innocent? He was going to put her away or probably handle it quietly himself? He wasn't that bad after all. He was actually one of the good guys. What has happened to me?

The room spun before Asher's eyes. The walls melted like candle wax. Scents shifted to nothing. All he heard was blood drip although he knew there was no fresh blood spilled.

At least not yet.

Drip

Drip.

Drip.

The floors cracked and split. The windows shattered. The books flew off the shelves. Diana and Theresa marbled together in an ebony and ivory Queen Chess piece,

twisting

and

turning into melted wax and blood.

What does a good man look like? Have I ever known?

Reality left him, and he stepped into some odd fantasy, something that would make the heaviest acid trip seem mild and childlike.

What is happening to me? Am I going crazy?

"No baby, you're not crazy," a voice said from the corner.

He spun and saw his mother, not as the woman he usually did, but the young, pretty version who cradled him in her arms. The version that sang beautiful lullabies before his bedtime. The woman who tucked him in under the covers instead of shoving him beneath the bed to hide.

The woman before all of those black eyes and tear-flooded days and alcohol induced anger and cracked ribs from being beat down by his dad, night after night.

"Mother?"

"Yes, darling. I'm here. It will all be okay." She reached out for him.

"What's happening?"

She enveloped Asher in a hug and stroked the back of his neck. "Oh, love. This is your reckoning. The moment where you accept the truth of who you are."

"Who am I, Mother? I don't know anymore."

Her lips brushed against his cheek and she whispered, "You're a monster. *My* monster."

Asher clenched his eyes together tightly and felt the threads that kept him tethered to reality–to the codes and morals and boundaries he set for himself. Snap. With each passing minute, Asher's chest rose with the blood that was on his hands. And when he opened his eyes, he zeroed in on Theresa.

"Asher?" Diana's voice sounded behind him.

He blocked her out and targeted Theresa with a sharpened gaze. "Do you know who I am?"

"You're Cupid." Her bottom lip shook.

"No, I'm a monster." Asher knocked her to the ground.

And then he did what monsters do best, he used his fists as if they were his bows, beat the tiny woman into a pulp.

Each strike was a hole to the chest, a sharp point that pierced flesh. Her screams rang in his ears like church bells signaling the time for service, and he was ready to come upon the lord and face his judgment,

but he'd do it, just like Jesus did,

he'd do it through blood.

"Asher, no!" Diana screamed. "Stop! Please, don't do this!"

It was Theresa's time to answer to God but there would be no service. Not for her. There would only be pain. And blood.

He struck her again and again and again, like a hammer to metal, the melody of her death rang out into the space.

Boom.

Boom.

Boom.

Boom.

He pummeled her head until it was mush and bone and blood and it stained his skin red and the lingering metallic scent coated his nostrils and his mouth, and even the cracked jagged edges of her skull scratched into his skin.

He never stopped.

"You're a monster." Am I? Why yes.

When he was finished with her head, he worked on the rest of her, clawing, biting, punching, ripping, and tearing the flesh of the small Asian woman.

"Asher! Stop! Stop!"

But he did not listen. He couldn't. For Diana would have to answer for her sins, too. And he was afraid of what his fists might do if she came any closer. He took it out on Theresa, what he couldn't do to Diana,

not yet,

but one day.

"Go, Diana. Now. Go to Flame. He'll drive you home."

"I can't leave you here. You're scaring me, Asher. Please, let me help—"

"Go! Before we both do something we'll regret." He stopped and glanced over his shoulder.

She met his gaze and it was there he saw her true fear. More visceral than any of the moments he'd shared with her. This was also her reckoning.

It's time we both realize the truth.

She wasn't in love with a man, she was in love with a monster. And there was no way she'd survive him.

Asher spent hours sitting next to Theresa's battered corpse. After a while, the blood and bones seemed to fade into the crimson stained carpet.

He'd vowed never to take a life that didn't deserve it and

there he was, sitting in his own lies. He had been so sure. So damn sure that Maxwell Grayson was a psychotic pedophile who ruined children's lives. And that poor man had begged and begged and begged.

And still, Asher hadn't believed him. His convictions wrapped up in the melody of Diana's demand.

Kill him, Asher. Please.

He'd done it for her as much as for himself. The way she gleamed at him when he said it was over. That Maxwell had been taken care of. The way her kisses and touches felt like a thank you to his soul. The way they made love with an idolized notion that Asher had killed one to save many.

And it was all a lie.

He cradled his head in his hands and shook.

His mother's voice rang in his head. "This is all her fault."

Not now.

Of all the times for his mother to show up, this was the worst of them all.

"Go away."

"I won't. You're hurting. I will heal you. That's what mothers are for." She slid next to him and put an arm around his shoulder.

"I didn't just kill that man, Mother. I tortured him. I left him no mercy and for what? For my stupidity? How can I possibly come back from this?"

"You don't. What's done is done. You must move on."

"Don't you see? I can't. I don't trust myself..."

She squeezed his arm tightly, her long nails digging into his flesh. "This is all *her* fault. She made you question everything! Asked you to do things you would never do for anyone else. She compromised you, Asher. And you let her!"

He looked into her eyes, "I love her. I would do anything for her."

"You really love her?" his mother asked.

Asher nodded.

"And you would do anything to save her?"

"Of course."

"Then, my dear son, you must die."

"But—"

"It's the only way, Asher. You knew this wouldn't last. It couldn't. You're a monster and she's a curious cat looking for answers. And she will find nothing but misery and heartbreak in you. I was a foolish woman, believing it was her that needed to die. But you will continue to suffer without her, Asher. It has to be you."

"I can't leave her. Not with this mess…"

His mother cackled. "You mean the mess she put you in? Of course you can."

She placed her hand on Asher's chest – where his heart would have been if he really thought he had one.

"It's time to come home to Momma, Asher. It's time to retire the bow and arrow and come back to me."

"Then who will protect everyone else?"

"Exactly."

"What are you saying?"

"This isn't a love story, darling. It never was. One of you has to die. Which one will it be? Are you Romeo or are you the bloody and lonely Macbeth?"

CHAPTER NINETEEN

ASHER

Hours later, Flame picked Asher up off the ground and loaded him into the limo.

He didn't know how long he'd sat in the filth of blood or next to Theresa's lifeless body, but he was certain death had seeped through his clothing and into his skin like a tattoo announcing his sins.

You must die.
You must die.
You must die.

He thought of Diana's cinnamon skin and the scent of roses bloomed in the backseat of the limo. He remembered the fullness of her breasts in his palms. The quiver in her thighs. The warmth and wetness of her cunt. His dick grew in his pants as all the parts of his beautiful Diana danced within her head.

But her brain. And her wit. And the tongue lashings she

gave him during their verbal sparring. Her determination for the truth. That is what made his cock throb in agony. That is what made his decision so damn hard.

I'll never feel her hand upon my chest or weave my hands through her black curls. I'll never get a nip of a sweet nipple or taste her pussy again. I'll die and be a fading memory to her. A ghost that haunts her for eternity. I can't do that to her.

He agonized over his mother's words. "It's the only way, Asher."

It couldn't be. There had to be another way. He would talk to Diana, let her wrap her arms around him and soothe the aches in his bones. She would take him into her, physically, emotionally and let him scratch out the fears within her flesh.

Diana would save him.

Somehow they would both survive it all.

CHAPTER TWENTY

DIANA

Diana fell asleep on the couch in the foyer after crying for hours. Grace had tried to comfort her, bring her food, pastries, and a blanket. Diana just wanted Asher. And forgiveness.

But she didn't know who to ask it from.

She hadn't believed in God since she found Gabby in her backyard. That was the moment she stopped believing. God wouldn't let that happen. He wouldn't let an innocent man go down for a crime he didn't commit, leaving his little girl behind to ponder the injustices of the world. God wouldn't create a man like Asher Bishop—a man who does bad things for the right reasons.

No, Diana didn't believe in God. But she prayed for redemption anyway.

And then she closed her eyes and wished that when she opened them—everything would be over.

But footsteps woke Diana up and nothing was over.

The door opened. Light shined in the darkened space.

Asher's huge frame took up the whole door way.

"Asher."

"Are you asleep?"

"I can't go to sleep."

"You should try."

"There's too much on my mind."

He sat down on the couch beside her, his hands running through his blonde curls, his blood-stained eyes straining to look at her. "Did you mean what you said earlier today?"

"What?"

"You called me a monster."

Suddenly, that image plowed into her head—Asher hammering into Theresa's dead body over and over. How could she not think he was a monster? Who did things like that? Even if he wanted justice, even if he hoped to save the world, a large part of him enjoyed killing people.

That was something she could not swallow.

That was what kept her up that night.

Tears glazed over Diana's eyes. She couldn't lie to him. He'd know it, and that would just make it all worse. She couldn't pretend. She could barely function after everything had occurred.

She, in fact, was a bird in a cage, and she couldn't figure out how to physically or even mentally escape.

There was no more hope.

"Yes," she whispered to him. "I meant it. You're a monster."

"How can you be so sure?"

"I watched you beat that woman like she was nothing."

"She wasn't nothing."

"She was a human being."

"She damaged lives."

"You killed an innocent man." She jabbed at his chest. "*You* damaged lives."

"Are you sure of this?"

"Yes."

"Sure enough like when you asked me to kill Maxwell?" he asked.

Diana shook her head and clenched her fists together. He didn't get to blame her completely. "Don't do this to me. I thought he was guilty, Asher. So. Did. You."

"I would have given him more time. I would have found the truth."

She reached for his hand. "You wanted to kill him before we even made it to the party. You're trying to pass the blame and I understand—"

He pushed her hand away and screamed, "You understand nothing! You haven't killed like I have! You haven't experienced the rush of blood and muscles and bone intersecting beneath your hands before. You've never watched the life go out a person's eyes, Diana. You. Know. Nothing."

She charged off the couch. "I know that you didn't really intend to kill the wrong person. I know that your heart is in the right place and that you're scared right now. I know you, Asher. The way I know myself. I won't pretend that I'm not afraid of you or that yes, I do think that you're a monster. You're not normal. You need help. But I want to give it to you. I want to find a way for us..."

He shook his head and turned away from her.

"Do you hear me?" She went to him, turned him around, placed her hand within his, and grazed his cheek with her other one. "I love you, Asher. I don't know if this could work, but... Jesus... what do you expect me to do? Run off with you and help you fight crime? I'm just a woman that's seen too much blood and it's all finally catching up to me."

He looked down at her. "We'll have to go our separate ways."

She sighed. "Is it really going to be that easy?"

Asher held her hands in his and closed his eyes. "No."

"Then tell me the truth," she whispered and held him close to her.

"One of us may not see tomorrow."

She shook against him. "Is that the only way?"

"I don't know." He kept the tears back. "I'm just the monster."

"Then, maybe it will work."

"How?"

"I don't know. I'm just so scared. Can't you stop? Can't you just get help or... I don't know, turn yourself in?"

"No. It feels too good."

"Don't say that."

"It does. I'm not just broken. I'm shattered, Diana."

"I'll put you back together."

"It doesn't work like that."

"Let me show you." Tears streamed down her face. Diana offered Asher her hand and led him to his bedroom, where they'd made love for the first time.

She prayed to a God she didn't believe in, that she could bring Asher back to her. That he would fill her with whatever goodness was left in him—so that she would be forgiven.

CHAPTER TWENTY-ONE

ASHER

Something had changed. Diana was no longer the medicine for his darkness. Instead, she'd caused the pain, and made the hunger for death even heavier to deal with.

No matter how many times Asher tried to push the desire for blood away, he craved it. The scent lingered on his skin. Metallic, coppery lust filled his senses.

As they made love, even Diana's lush, velvet skin couldn't distract him. He trembled with the need to kill again.

And again.

You're a monster. You must die.

"Asher?"

Diana's voice pulled him out of his thoughts.

"What?" He blinked at her.

"Stop thinking and make love to me. Your body is here, but your mind is somewhere else." She turned his chin toward her. "Look at me. We'll figure this out."

He shook his head. "Why aren't you running away from me? I'm evil."

She cupped his face in her hands. "No, Asher. You made a mistake. We both did. We'll get through this. Together."

He buried his head in her chest. She had so much faith in him and he didn't deserve it. Even after all she knew of him, she still gave him all of herself. He'd never find that in a woman ever again.

She pushed him down, kissing him on the lips. She held onto his hands and squeezed as her kisses intensified.

Yet, every few seconds, between the moans and her screams of pleasure, fear twitched at the edge of her eyes. There was no denying it. She didn't look like she wanted to fuck him. Diana was scared out of her mind and had shifted into survival mode.

Or was it all just in his head?

"Do you want this?" He sucked on her neck.

"Yes, baby. I need this."

"Are you sure?"

"Yes."

"Okay."

Lust rushed through him. In seconds, the sensations of her body warmed around his, and all control left him. He was barely holding on and ready to explode.

Instantly, Asher melted into Diana's touch. He never wanted to let this go—this meeting of their two bodies. He wanted it to go on forever.

Diana eased herself on his thickening cock, so slowly he groaned out.

"Yes," she whispered. "Take it out on me, Asher."

He shook his head. "No."

She bit his bottom lip. "You sacrificed for me. Now it's my turn. Do it!"

What? This wasn't Diana.

She was giving herself to him for the taking. "You can do whatever you like, okay. I-I'll be your anchor. I'll make it all better."

Doubt pinched at him.

She wants to take away my pain? Absolve me of my guilt? Numb me? Fix me? She loves me? Or is she afraid of the monster?

He eased Diana off of him and flipped her onto her stomach.

Never will I fall in love again.

He closed his eyes and guided himself into her.

She was tight.

So fucking pleasurable he almost came in seconds.

Diana...

And he kissed the length of her spine before thrusting into her hard.

With every moan that escaped her lips, he let a tear fall. His mother was right—things could never last between them. Not the way things were. He would ruin her and that was the last thing he wanted. He'd rather be dead than see Diana turn into someone she wasn't.

She should be preserved as the goddess she was—the woman who loved him despite his flaws. But it would never last. She'd learn to hate him. Resent him. Blame him for

Neil's death. Her fall from grace and mental stability. The blood would be too much. The fear would corrode all the things that he loved about her. She'd try to escape either by running away or drowning in alcohol and pills.

And there was no alternative to letting her go. She'd tell one day. It would happen. Whether to the police or just a confession to a trusty friend. She'd have to tell because the guilt would hurt too much and destroy her life.

Diana.

Asher clung to her waist as he thrust his dick into her over and over again. He memorized the way her hair fell in ringlets onto her back. The way her breasts moved in harmony to his thrusts.

He watched her hands grasp for the edge of the bed and let the shape of her fingers and wrist burn into his memory.

He had to remember it all,

the shape of her ass, ripe and formed just for him.

The feel of her cunt as he moved in and out.

"Oh! Asher, don't stop."

"I love you, Diana." When Asher was close to spilling his seed into her, he flipped her onto her back and entered her missionary so that he could kiss her lips one more time. "I'll always love you."

He wanted every inch of Diana to be scorched in his brain.

His memory.

Just in case.

"Oh, Fuck, Asher. I'm coming!" she screamed, her legs

and arms trembling around him.

"Yes, baby." Asher plowed into her, his orgasm reaching him as Diana's ended. When it was over, he collapsed beside her and kissed her lips. Her cheeks.

There's no other way...

His mother's words rang in his ears and let it replay over and over again until he knew it to be the truth. He knew what he needed to do to save them both.

Asher sat up and Diana placed a hand on his chest. "Are you okay?"

"No." He kissed her on the forehead. "I love you, Diana. Don't you ever forget."

She smiled. "I know you do. I love you, too."

"Then you'll forgive me," he mumbled under his breath and got up from the bed.

"What did you say?" she asked.

But there was really nothing else to say.

He entered his closet, walked to the back, and grabbed his bow and arrows.

How long had he used this bow to kill? Ten carved lines decorated the handle, but since he'd met Diana, he'd forgot to update them.

In the darkness of his closet, all the way in the back, he turned around. Diana sat on the bed, unable to see him, just like the first time he'd met her, and sat in the shadows of the kitchen with her dead husband on the floor.

The bow was carbon, barely three pounds, and with a leather grip. Blood always came, when Asher drew back his bow. The arrows were fast and easy to pull, and oh how he loved to make them fly.

And tonight would be no different.

"I'm not Cupid." He positioned the bow and targeted Diana's chest. "I'm a monster."

CHAPTER TWENTY-TWO

GRACE

Grace's boss, Asher Bishop looked dashing in his charcoal gray suit and his blonde curls slicked back. It had been weeks since he'd even been dressed and out of his bed before lunch.

She didn't know what happened. First, he'd been love struck and with that Mrs. Carson every second of the day—them making love so loud the whole staff could hear them down stairs.

And then the poor girl never came around anymore. Mrs. Carson stopped visiting. The news reported her missing, and Mr. Bishop had gone into a zombie state, barely eating or sleeping, just drinking all night and arguing with his dead mother.

But today, healing had shown. He'd gotten out of bed, put his clothes on, and come down stairs like the old Mr. Bishop used to do. Even, his blue eyes sparkled against the sunlight filtering into the dining room.

A smile spread over Grace's lips.

I really hope they find that girl. She's been missing for weeks.

Humming that strange little lullaby that he always had on his tongue, he kept the Ovid Island Newspaper in one hand and his coffee in the other.

"Good morning, Mr. Bishop."

"He looked up from his newspaper and winked. "Good morning, my lovely and amazing Grace."

"Wow. You're in a great mood today."

"I had a delicious amount of loving this morning." He chuckled to himself and then shook his head. "Okay, Diana. Okay. I'm sorry. I didn't mean to tell Grace about our hot love session this morning."

A laugh fled his lips.

Grace edged away, and looked around the room, wondering if she'd finally gone crazy. After being in the Bishop house for so many years, maybe it was her turn to go insane. Lose her marbles. Lord knows there's been more than enough crazy floating around the Bishop Mansion in the last decade for it to have rubbed off on Grace.

Only Asher and she sat in the room. Every other seat at the table was empty.

"Will you just accept my apology, Diana?" Asher blew a kiss to the empty chair on his right. "Yes, my love. Yes. I know."

Lord have mercy. Now he's talking to Mrs. Carson. Let me get out of here before I have to start serving JFK and Marilyn Monroe. Who knows who else is sitting up in this room with this crazy man?

"You look lovely today, Grace." He smiled at her.

"Thank you, sir." She fell into her calming habit, and patted the pocketknife she had in her apron. There was a tube of mace tucked in her bra as well as a cross with Jesus's image right in the center.

Mr. Bishop never gave her a reason to think he would attack her, besides the fact that he was absolutely insane.

"And the spread this morning is absolutely delightful." He turned to his left. "What do you think, Mother?"

Oh Jesus. His mother is here too? Well, how does she like Mrs. Carson? I bet she hates her. That woman is always rude and... What am I saying? She's dead, and that poor girl... well she might be too.

Grace stared at Asher for longer than she should have.

Two women that this man loves are both ghosts in his dining room. That's either really bad luck or... well... that's some coincidence.

"Okay, Mother. We've got it. You don't like Grace, but have some respect for her." He turned to Grace. "I for one, appreciate everything that you do for me. Please, keep it up."

"Thank you, sir. I will." She refilled his coffee cup. "Is there anything else you need from me?"

"No, but maybe Diana would want something." Asher directed his attention to her empty seat. "Diana? Would you like another muffin?"

He chuckled at something and turned to his left. "Mother, would you please calm yourself. Grace has always obliged you. I'm talking to Diana now."

I'm going to have to turn that resignation in tomorrow. One ghost was bad enough to serve, now I have two. I don't get paid that much. And all that food that I waste every day. This is crazy.

Asher looked at Grace with sorrowful eyes. "I'm sorry for my mother's absurd reactions to things, Grace. You know how she is."

He tilted Grace's way and whispered, "And frankly, now that Mother is meeting Diana, both women are vying for my attention."

Grace stared at both empty chairs and then back at him. "Mrs. Carson..."

"Yes, Grace?" he asked.

"Mrs. Carson would you like something?"

Asher shook his head. "Diana, you have to speak louder."

A deranged laugh fled from his lips and made Grace jump.

"Okay. Okay." Asher shook his head. "You funny girl. I will leave you alone."

Asher turned back to Grace.

"What did she say?" Grace asked as the coffeepot shook in her hands.

Asher quirked his eyebrows at the woman as if she'd lost her mind. "Diana already told you what she wanted, but fine, I can say it again. Are all of you are going crazy this morning? Women!"

He chuckled. "Diana would like another orange juice and

perhaps one of your cranberry scones. She's feeling feisty today."

"Y-Yes sir." Grace bowed and left the room.

When she entered the kitchen she nearly dropped the coffeepot to the floor. Caught it before it shattered and set it on the counter before grabbing the phone from the wall and dialing a number.

"He's talking to ghosts again," Grace whispered into the phone. "I don't know that I can do this. Mrs. Bishop was hard enough, Flame. But Mrs. Carson? She was real! Flesh and blood and bones and tears."

Flame shushed her. "We will do what we have to and help him get through this. He's just dealing with Mrs. Carson's disappearance terribly."

"You think? He's talking to two empty chairs."

"Grace, relax."

"I don't know if I can do this anymore. I'm thinking about turning in my resignation."

"Who else could help him with this?"

"There are hundreds of chefs that are out of work and will get these huge paychecks to deal with this crazy man."

"But none are you, Grace. Do you need more money?"

"I need him to get some help."

"He will, and what do you know, Mrs. Carson may be discovered, and all will be well."

"The police think that Cupid got her."

"Who knows what happened to her. All we can do is focus on the problem at hand. Who should we be considering?"

"Mr. Bishop," she mumbled.

"Yes, we need to focus on Mr. Bishop."

She sighed. "You're right. Thank you. You've always been my voice of reason in this nutty household."

"I try." Flame lowered his voice a little. "But, Grace, if you find the rest of the staff having these same problems, let me know. We need to make sure that everyone on the estates are helping him out through this rough time."

"Okay."

Flame hung up on her and she wiped away tears that she hadn't realized were on her face. Sometimes the craziness of a job could just get to the core of a person, and rip the sanity right out of them. Things had to change. Flame might've been right that the whole staff as well as Grace should stand by him, but in the end,

crazy was crazy,

and sometimes crazy people kill the normal ones around them.

"The Lord is my shepherd." Grace straightened up and smoothed out her apron. "I shall not want."

She cleared her throat and headed back.

"Mr. Bishop, would Mrs. Carson or Mrs. Bishop like some other pastries?" Grace asked as she returned to the dining room with a fresh pot of coffee.

OVID ISLAND
REPORTER

CUPID'S LATEST VICTIM

Diana Carson, fellow contributor to the Ovid Island Reporter, was discovered inside of her apartment with an arrow to the heart and an apparent message from the serial killer she had been invesigating - Cupid.

I'm Sorry.

Ovid Island Police are still investigating whether Mrs. Carson had knowledge of Cupid's identity or was close to figuring out who he was and caused her untimely demise.

Diana Carson

Mrs. Carson was known for her blistering honesty and dedication to the truth.

May she rest in peace.

VALENTINE PLAYLIST

Listen to the playlist on Spotify

Meg Myers – Desire

The Weeknd – Earned It

Sofia Karlberg – Crazy in Love

Ellie Goulding – Love Me Like You Do

Bebe Rexha – I'm Gonna Show You Crazy

Chelsea Lankes – Secret

Zack Hemsey – Vengeance

Broods – Sleep Baby Sleep

Melanie Martinez – Dead To Me

Iron & Wine – Such Great Heights

City and Colour – What Makes A Man

Eels – Love Of The Loveless

Gotye – Eyes Wide Open

Joshua Radin – Only You

Justin Nozuka – Save Him

Stars – Dead Hearts

KENYA WRIGHT

Writer. Lover. **Foodie**. Mother. **Book Addict.**
Masturbator. **Comedian.** Super Hero. **Blogger.** Professional
Adventurer.

ALSO BY KENYA WRIGHT

Series

Chasing Love (Interracial Erotic Romance)

An Arrangement of Love (Chasing Love #1)

A Test of Love (Chasing Love #2)

Bad for You (Interracial Dark Erotic Adventure Romance)

Bad for You 1: Sexual Deception

Bad for You 2: The Deadly Game

Bad for You 3: The Final Play

Bad for You Trilogy Boxed Set

Santeria Habitat Series (Dark Urban Fantasy/ Horror Romance)

Caged View (Book .5)

Fire Baptized (Book 1)

The Burning Bush (Book 2)

Wildfire Gospel (Book 3)

The Vampire King Series

Escape (Book 1)

Captured (Book 2)

Freed (Book 3)

Coventon Campus Series (Interracial Erotic Romance)

Complicated by You (Book 1)

Committed To You (Book 2)

Erotic Elf Series (Erotic Paranormal Romance)

Incubus Hunter (Book 1)

Billionaire Games Series (New Adult Erotic Romance)

Theirs to Play (Book 1)

Standalones

Chameleon

Flirting with Chaos

No Ordinary Love

The Babysitter (New Adult Erotic Short)

The Muse (Interracial Romantic Suspense)

Sexy as Sin (Interracial Erotic Romance)

JADE EBY

Once upon a time there was a little girl who fell in love with books then she grew up to write her own.

ALSO BY JADE EBY

Series

Back to Bad Series

Capricious (Book 1)

Voracious (Book 2)

Malicious (Book 3)

Audacious (Book 4)

Tenacious (Book 5)

Lacey: The Back to Bad Series Bundle

Whiskey and a Gun & The Finish Companions

Whiskey and a Gun

The Finish

Dirty Proof (Combined Whiskey and a Gun + The
Finish + Bonus Material)

Standalones

The Right Kind of Wrong

Stuck: A Free Short Story for Newsletter Subscribers

Things We Never Say (not yet available for the public)

Made in the USA
Monee, IL
19 November 2023

46897386R00163